P9-CMO-299

Meranda and the Legend of the Lake

Owlkids Books acknowledges the financial support of the Canada Council for the Arts, the Ontario Arts Council, the Government of Canada through the Canada Book Fund (CBF) and the Government of Ontario through the Ontario Creates Book Initiative for our publishing activities.

Published in Canada by Owlkids Books Inc.
1 Eglinton Avenue East, Toronto, ON M4P 3A1

Published in the United States by Owlkids Books Inc.
1700 Fourth Street, Berkeley, CA, 94710

Library of Congress Control Number: 2021930576

Library and Archives Canada Cataloguing in Publication

Title: Meranda and the legend of the lake / by Meagan Mahoney.
Names: Mahoney, Meagan, author.
Identifiers: Canadiana 20210110724 | ISBN 9781771474344 (hardcover)
Classification: LCC PS8626.A4174155 M47 2021 | DDC jC813/.6—dc23

Edited by Sarah Howden | Design by Alisa Baldwin

Manufactured in Altona, MB, Canada, in May 2021, by Friesens
Job #273956

A B C D E F

Publisher of Chirp, Chickadee and OWL
www.owlkidsbooks.com

Meranda and the Legend of the Lake

By
MEAGAN MAHONEY

Owlkids Books

For Grace.

May your life always be filled with stories . . .

and a touch of magic.

“We two have paddled in the stream,
from morning sun till dine;
But seas between us broad have roared
since days of long ago.”

—Robert Burns

Chapter 1

I don't get butterflies in my stomach, I get tempests. Anything from thunderstorms to violent swells. Tonight, my anticipation is a full-blown hurricane. We leave tomorrow morning on a six a.m. flight. I know I'm not supposed to be as excited as I am. It *is* a funeral after all, but if that's what it takes, so be it.

Mom got the call during dinner on Sunday. It was Gran. That was weird because with the three-hour time difference, she hardly ever calls us in the evenings. Mom must have known something was up because she ducked into the den to take the call. Her voice was low, and there were lots of long pauses. Dad and I stopped eating and stared at the closed door to the den. Each of us tried to guess what was being said on the other side.

When Mom opened the door, her red eyes locked with Dad's. Her face was pale and serious.

"Uncle Mark," she said. "They think he had a heart attack on the boat. Mom said the crew did what they could, but they never got him back."

Dad got up from the table, wiped his hands on his napkin, and put his arms around Mom. "I'm so sorry, Beth. How's your mom?"

"Shocked. Numb, I think."

Uncle Mark is, or was, I guess, Mom's uncle. My great-uncle. He's been out here to visit a few times, usually when Gran and Grampa come, and we talk, or *talked,* over video chat on the weekends when he was at Gran's for dinner. I remember one time he did a whole magic show for me with props and everything. Another time he taught me how to tie sailor's knots. I used a shoelace. He was a pretty cool old guy. Mom always called him her favorite uncle. He never had any kids of his own, so I guess he decided he didn't have to grow up.

"I told him they should have an AED on board. I think I must have had that conversation with him a hundred times. If they're out beyond the bay and something happens, there's nothing they can do about it until they get back to shore. Damn fishing industry. Think they're invincible."

Mom's an ER doctor. She thinks most "accidents" are preventable.

"What do you want to do?" Dad asked, searching Mom's face.

"I … I don't … I think I have to go. Not only for me, but for Mom."

"I think we should all go," Dad said slowly, holding her gaze.

I held my breath. I didn't want to move in case they remembered I was there. I think it worked because then Dad said: "It's been long enough now, Beth. It'll be okay."

Mom drew a long, ragged breath. "Do you really think so?" Her eyes filled with fresh tears, and she gripped Dad's arm. "What about—? I just don't know if—?"

"Beth, we *need* to go back. It's time. Time to go home."

Mom nodded, resigned, but if I didn't know better, I'd say she looked more worried than sad.

Chapter 2

Home. It's funny how "home" can mean different places for different people. Even in the same family. Home for me is Calgary, Alberta. Mountains, prairies, big skies, and bright sunshine. Home for Mom and Dad is Nova Scotia. Dad grew up outside of Halifax, and Mom's from Cape Breton, a big island on the northeast coast of the province. Fishing, fog, tides, and water. It's a place I have imagined for as long as I can remember.

I'm finishing up my packing. Mom is downstairs, crossing items off her list as she puts stuff in her suitcase.

"Don't forget to pack a pair of tights to go with your dress, Meranda. It may be chilly this week," Mom calls up. "And make sure you bring elastics and a hairband or something to get your hair off your face for the funeral, okay?"

"Got it, Mom."

I hear the front door close when Dad gets home. "Hello?

Everyone packed and ready?" He tries to joke with Mom about her neurotic packing habits. I don't hear a laugh.

"Did you get things tidied up at the lab?" she asks. Dad's a cancer scientist at the university. He's going to find a cure one day, I'm sure of it. He's the smartest person I know, even if he does tell the worst jokes.

"Pretty much," he answers. "I'll keep in touch with them while we're away. Should be fine. What can I do to help?"

I hear Mom sending Dad off to gather the final things from her list.

I grab my crumpled copy of *Legends of the Lakes* from my bedside table to pack. Gran and Grampa gave me this book when I was little, and for years its chapters were the only bedtime stories I wanted to hear. It's written by a woman in Mom's hometown, which is famous for mermaids. Yep, mermaids—or mermaid legends, at least, and this book is a chronicle of them all. I know most of the stories by heart, but when Gran visits, I still let her read it aloud to me. It makes her happy. And maybe me too. A little. I smooth the bent edges of the cover and tuck it in the last pocket of space in my backpack on top of my math notebook.

Mrs. Jackson said I wouldn't miss much with this being only the second week of school, but Mom insisted I get some homework to bring with me. "Wouldn't want to fall behind!" Not a worry there. In fact, the thought of being a bit behind in class would be a relief for a while. Don't get me wrong, I love school. Like *really* love school. But I'm learning that in seventh grade, that's not normal—and, with a December birthday, I'm always the youngest in my class, which doesn't help either. I wonder sometimes if I didn't try so hard then maybe the other kids would like me more. I know that sounds pathetic. Especially since in every other area of my life I can never quite keep up. My crutches always ensure I'm a few steps behind—in gym, in the hallways, at recess. Somehow, being extra quick at math doesn't make up for my physical limitations. Not that anyone is mean to me or anything, but no matter what I do, I seem to float through life a bit out of step. In my dreams, I can fly or swim faster than everyone (no crutches needed either way). But when I'm awake, I'm Meranda Morgan—smart, slow-moving, quiet, mostly invisible.

Invisible to everyone except my parents, of course. There's no floating by them. Some kids have helicopter parents; I think of mine as seatbelt parents. They don't just hover, they hold me tight to keep me safe and close. Sometimes it gets a bit much, like when the seatbelt locks and you can't move. Or breathe. Apparently, this is normal for an only child, especially one with physical challenges, but sometimes I'm not so sure.

I zip up my bag and get ready for bed. I'm brushing my teeth when Mom comes up behind me and kisses the top of my head. "All ready to go?" she asks.

I spit. "Yup. You?"

"Almost," she says. "I still have to make a final decision on an outfit for the funeral. Then we'll see how well we can all sleep tonight."

Our faces are side by side in the mirror. Mom's normally sparkling blue eyes are dim, like she's fogged in. Her red hair is frizzy and wisps of it have managed to escape from her ponytail and tickle the freckles on her cheeks. Next to her, I look like I have a suntan—my dark hair and dark eyes accentuate the darkness of my skin. The thick lenses of my glasses make my eyes look bigger than they actually are. We couldn't look more different, but as Mom always says, "We're kindred on the inside, and that's all that counts." Tonight, the lines on her face are more obvious than usual, her cheeks are pale, and she moves like she's underwater: heavy and slow. My heart swells, and I feel like a jerk for being excited when clearly she's so sad.

"I love you, Mom. I know this is going to be hard for you." I look at her in the mirror.

"Thanks, sweetie. Love you more."

"Love you most," I say with a wink. It's a silly routine we've had since I was little. Arguing about who loves who more.

She smiles. "G'night." And one more kiss on my head.

I make my way back to my room and take my arms out of my crutches to lean them up against my dresser. My legs are extra tight tonight. They don't usually hurt much, but there's not quite enough room for me and my crutches to shuffle from dresser to closet and back so many times. So there was a lot of pivoting, leaning, and short steps without crutches while I was packing, and I'm feeling it now. I sit on the edge of my bed to rub my calves, trying to massage some of the stiffness away.

I crawl under the covers and hug my arms tightly around myself to stop from exploding into a million pieces. Nervous. Excited. Sad. All of it. I pull my duvet up to my chin and roll over onto my side so I can see the painting on the wall by the window. Gran and Grampa gave it to me when I was a baby so I would "always know where my roots are." The waves look like they're reaching for the rocks on the shoreline, for something to hold on to. The gray clouds are dotted with the pinkish orange of the approaching sunset or sunrise. Sometimes I imagine the sun is about to come up after a terrible ocean storm and with the sun comes calm. Other times, the sun is about to set, and the tempest is growing as darkness takes over. Tonight, it's the former. I swallow my nerves and focus on the sandy part of the shoreline. I imagine, as I have so many times, the sound of the waves cresting when the bubbles splash my ankles, my feet sinking into the rough sand.

I must have drifted off to sleep at some point because I wake to Mom and Dad whispering in the hall. It's still dark. Dad pokes his head into my room.

"You awake, kiddo?"

"Just," I manage through a yawn.

"Leave in twenty minutes?" he says. "We'll grab something to eat at the airport."

"'Kay."

I throw off my covers and get out of bed as fast as I can.

By tonight I'll be in Cape Breton.

Home.

Chapter 3

"The captain has turned on the seatbelt sign. Please fasten your seatbelts and return your seats to the full upright position in preparation for landing."

"Who will pick us up at the airport?" I ask Mom as I gather my things, putting my book and headphones into my backpack. "How long is the drive to Gran and Grampa's place? When can we go out in the boat? Do they really have their own dock right on the lake? Can we go to the gift shop? The one Gran says has the mermaid scales?"

Mom gives me a tired smile and does her best to answer my thousand questions, most of which I already know the answers to. As she talks, she picks at her cuticles. She does this when she's nervous and I notice that she already has Band-Aids on three of her fingers.

My parents moved to Calgary from Cape Breton when I was

three. Mom got a job in the emergency department at the new children's hospital that was too good to turn down. That was eight years ago. I've never been back to Cape Breton. There are three main reasons I've been given for this. Number one: it's far. This is fair, but we've traveled to farther places on vacations in the past few years. Number two: our extended family loves spending time with us out West, so we see them lots. No need to make the trek to the East right now. This is also fair. We have a nearly constant stream of relatives visiting and the mountains are pretty fun. Number three: my safety. Gran and Grampa's house is on a point of land on the Bras d'Or Lake. It's surrounded by water, and Mom worries that it's not a safe place for a little kid. I've tried to argue this, since she somehow managed to survive growing up there, and I'm not a "little kid" anymore, but I can't win this one.

Here is the thing about Mom: as an emergency doc at a children's hospital, she sees some pretty awful stuff. Because of this, she has some very firm rules. No trampolines (lots of broken bones), hot dogs always cut lengthwise (a few terrible cases of choking), and God help me if she were to ever see me on my bike or skis without a helmet! But water is her biggest fear. Swimming lessons in a safe pool with lifeguards, absolutely. Paddling at a sandy beach by a (very) small, calm lake, maybe.

Waves? No. Ocean? No way. "It's just not worth the risk," she says, or the impossible-to-argue-with "You're my one and only very precious child. What would I ever do if I lost you?" And the conversation-stopping "I'm not sure that your legs would be strong enough if you were to go under."

Grampa is waiting for us at the bottom of the escalator by the baggage claim. I spot the red rooster ball cap we sent him for Father's Day last year as I ride down. When I reach the bottom, I make my way to his embrace as fast as my legs will carry me.

"Hiya, girlie. Boy, I think you've grown since the beginning of the summer." His whiskers scratch my cheek, and I smell the dirt from the garden on his clothes. "I'm so happy you're here," he says, ruffling my hair. "I wish it were for a happier reason, but the sight of you sure has put some sunshine in my heart. And I know it definitely will for Gran."

"Hi, Dad." Mom drops her bag and buries her head in Grampa's flannel shirt.

"My girl," he whispers. "So glad you're here." He kisses her forehead, and when he smiles at her, the lines in his forehead seem deeper than before. Mom wipes her cheeks with her sleeve and picks up her purse from the floor.

"Hi, Bill," Dad says, shaking Grampa's hand. "Thanks so much for coming to get us."

"Good to see you, Gabe. To tell you the truth, it was kinda nice to have a reason to leave that house for a few hours. Lots going on to get ready for Thursday. Gonna be a pretty big funeral, I expect. Who knew the guy had so many friends?" Grampa grins and winks at me.

Dad and Grampa pile our luggage into Grampa's truck. Mom and I sit together in the back, and Dad gets into the passenger seat next to Grampa.

Mom takes my hand and gives it a squeeze. Turning it over, she moves her fingers to the inside of my wrist and traces the outline of my birthmark. "So here we are," she whispers.

The bumpy pink splotch on the inside of my arm looks like a loonie-sized island. I rub it when I'm anxious or nervous. I don't even notice I'm doing it. Dad jokes that Cape Breton left its mark on me. Literally. Like a stamp telling the world where I'm from. I joke that I should just write "return to sender" on my arm so I can finally get to visit. Mom's never found that very funny.

It's three and a half hours to Gran and Grampa's place from the airport. Through Nova Scotia, across the Canso Causeway, and onto the island. Mom, Dad, and Grampa are chatting about the details of the funeral, and I am glued to the window.

Dad looks over his shoulder at me and says, "No real ocean views until the causeway, kiddo. The first part of the drive is mostly inland. Why don't you close your eyes for a bit, and I'll wake you when we get a view?"

As if. "I don't think I can sleep, Dad. Grampa, are we going to drive by the school? And the pier?" Gran used to be a teacher. She even taught Mom since the town was too small to have more than one class for each grade. Grampa was a boat mechanic, so he spent lots of time with the fishermen and their equipment on the pier. My family's history is like a fairy tale to me. Stories and places that have existed only in my imagination. I can't wait to see how close my imagined scenes are to reality.

"Don't fret, my girl," Grampa says. "I'll give you the royal tour while you're here."

"Let's see how much time we have, Dad, okay? Let's not forget what we're all here for," Mom says.

I run through the list in my mind of the places I want Grampa to take me. The school, the pier, the bakery, the lighthouse … and eventually the lull of the car rocks me to sleep.

Rolling. Bobbing. Swaying.

Silence.

Bubbles escape my nostrils. My hair floats around my head like a web. My limbs move slowly but easily though the water, propelled by a gentle current. I look down and notice that I am holding someone's hand. I look upward for a face and …

"Meranda. Sweetie, wake up. Have a look out your window." Mom squeezes my hand. I blink and stretch the horrible crick in my neck. We're crossing over the causeway. Ocean on both sides of the car. For a few brief moments, I am actually *in* the ocean—surrounded by water. It's windy and the waves are crashing up on the rocks beside the road. I roll down my window to let the sound wash over me. A gust of salt air blasts into the car, and my face is moist from the mist. I gulp in the taste and close my eyes, and for a moment I am back in my dream.

"Ooooh, honey, it's a bit windy to keep the window open!" Mom smiles and brushes the moist curls from my forehead. "Close it for now, okay?"

The rest of the drive is speckled with big hills and views of the lake. For as far back as my memory can reach, I've imagined the Bras d'Or Lake. Grampa calls it the Cape Breton Sea because it's so big. It's like a giant hole in the middle of the island, and it's part freshwater and part saltwater, so it's pretty unique. Grampa says its name comes from the way the sun bounces in a golden shimmer off the waves. "Bras" means arm in French, and "Or" means gold. Arms of Gold. The shoreline is wrapped by the hills in a green rolling embrace in some parts, and in other parts I can't even see the land on the other side.

Grampa turns the truck off the highway and drives inland,

away from the lake. Some of the trees in the forest on either side of the road are dappled with red or orange.

"We're here!" I announce when I spot a big wooden sign through the windshield. "Welcome to Skye," it reads in dark blue letters, and below, "Home of the Bras d'Or Mermaids." Next to the words is an image of a mermaid waving. Her tail extends below the letters and wraps around the bottom of the sign.

"Almost home," Grampa says.

The road veers left and opens up onto the town's main street (it's really more of a village, actually, considering how tiny this stretch is). We have an old photo of this street in our kitchen in Calgary. It is so familiar to me that I'm surprised when we drive through and the buildings move past my window, like they should only exist in a snapshot in a frame, still and faded. But the street is anything but, with storefronts vividly painted in blues and reds and yellows, each one unique. We pass two mermaid-themed gift shops on the short block that is the downtown, then a coffee shop, a diner, the post office, and the library before turning off Main Street.

"That was it," says Dad. "Skye. Blink, and you'll miss it!" He laughs and looks back and winks at Mom. She doesn't seem to notice.

We turn onto a dirt road that winds around the point. Then

the driveway with the painted sign out front: The Campbells. The words *dìon maighdeann-mhara* are painted beneath. I know from my mermaid book that this means "mermaid's protection" in Gaelic, but also because it was the opening line in every bedtime story my grandparents told me when I was little. The legends of the Bras d'Or Mermaids were my favorite fairy tales, and I hear the ancient phrase like a lullaby in my mind as I whisper the words aloud. The house comes into view through a crop of crab apple trees. A large two-story cottage with gray wooden siding and a white porch that hugs it all around. Before we even open the doors of the car, Gran is on the porch with arms spread wide. I grab my crutches from the seat beside me, run to her, and am wrapped in the warm smell of cinnamon from her flowered apron.

"Finally," she says under her breath. "Welcome home, Meranda." She kisses the top of my head and hugs me once more before reaching for Mom.

"Hi, honey." She puts her hand on Mom's arm, and I see tears jump to her eyes. They share a sad smile. Gran rubs Mom's arm gently. "Thank you for coming. This is going to be all right. You'll see." She speaks slowly, her eyes locked on Mom's.

Mom inhales deeply and nods her head. I can barely make out the words she breathes. "I sure hope you're right."

Chapter 4

Gran and Grampa's house is exactly as I imagined. I guess it wasn't all my imagination—FaceTime may have had something to do with it. But even the smells are familiar. Like a swirl of flowers, cinnamon, and wood. As the screen door closes, I turn to see the vastness of the lake open up in front of us through the floor-to-ceiling windows in the living room at the back of the house. The sky is just starting to turn pink, and I can see the silhouettes of a few sailboats against a coastline lit by the setting sun. It's like my painting. Only calmer.

"Don't be shy, girl, come on in," Grampa says behind me. He gives my arm a squeeze and leads me to the windows. From there I have a view of the deck that extends across the back of the house and the gazebo on the edge of the yard. We're surrounded by trees, and in a small clearing I can make out the top of a railing that disappears over the edge toward the water.

“Are those steps?” I ask Grampa.

Before he can answer, Mom is at my side. And before she can say anything, I blurt out, “I know, I know. Off-limits, right?”

Mom closes her eyes for a few seconds and takes a deep breath. “Maybe let’s not argue about this tonight, Meranda? It’s been a long day of travel and an emotional week. I’m not sure I can handle worrying about you on the dock right now.” Her shoulders slump a little, and she closes her eyes again in a long blink. I can’t help but think she looks a little defeated. So I retreat.

“Sorry, Mom. That didn’t come out right. I just meant you don’t have to tell me. I know the rules.”

“Maybe I’ll be able to take you down to the dock tomorrow, if we’re not needed for family stuff,” offers Grampa cautiously.

“Bill …” starts Gran. “Let’s see what the next few days bring, shall we?”

Mom seems happy enough with that for now. She has gone back into the kitchen and is sitting up at the countertop fidgeting with a pen next to a notepad. “Will Reverend Tim be performing the service?” she asks Gran, glancing at the pad. And with that, the funeral is the focus, not me. Mom and Gran huddle over the “To Do” list in the kitchen while Dad helps Grampa unload the groceries Grampa picked up in Halifax.

I take the opportunity for some time to myself, to wander the house and see how much of it matches what I imagined. My crutches thump on the honey-colored wood floor, then are silent as I move farther into the living room and onto the braided rug. The house feels familiar and cozy. From the wooden furniture that Grampa made with love to the antique grandfather clock on the wall in front of the stairs, I know this place as though I've been here a thousand times.

I look up at the clock, surprised for a moment at the time. The three-hour difference slipped my mind. The two wood-carved mermaids that frame the clockface stare down from their post high above my head. I run my fingers along the glass protecting the pendulum. It's a brass fish tail with thousands of scales that glisten when it swings from side to side like light reflecting on the surface of the lake. It is mesmerizing and even more beautiful in real life than over a computer screen.

The clock is a family heirloom. It has been in Gran's family forever and is apparently quite a famous part of town folklore. It has its own chapter in the *Legends* book. Uncle Mark told me the story many, many times. It was made by Gran's great-grandfather, Malcolm McKenzie, who had been a watchmaker in Scotland. When he came to Canada, the ship he was traveling on was caught in a great storm. The ship capsized, and hundreds of souls were lost. Some managed to clamber into lifeboats and were rescued the next morning by another passing vessel. Malcolm did not make it into a boat. He was thrown into the water as the ship went down.

"He thought he was a goner. Preparing to meet ol' Davy Jones." I can hear Uncle Mark telling the story like he's standing beside me. "But then ... he woke up on the sand. On the shore of the lake. Covered in kelp. *Alive.*"

It's an amazing (or crazy) story for sure, but the most unbelievable part is where they found him. On the shore of Bras d'Or Lake. This is hard to imagine since the ship had gone down in the North Atlantic, and the distance from there through the channel to the lake is far. Like not he-floated-to-shore far but that's-impossible far. The only explanation Malcolm had for his miraculous survival was—wait for it—mermaids. For the rest of his days, he was known as Merman McKenzie, and he swore up and down that mermaids saved his life. He spent a decade creating the clock as a sort of tribute to his saviors.

Watching the tail swing slowly and rhythmically like waves splashing and retreating, my eyes are suddenly heavy.

"I think we'd better get you some rest." Dad is beside me. "It's been a long day and we were all up pretty early." He puts his hand on my shoulder.

For once, I don't argue. My legs are heavy; sleep is closing in.

"Goodness! Of course you're exhausted, sweetheart," says Gran from the kitchen, wiping her hands on her apron. "I'll take you upstairs and help you get settled. I think you'll be comfortable up there."

"G'night, Meranda. Love you so much." Mom kisses my cheek.

"Sleep well, kiddo."

"G'night, Dad."

I hug Mom and Dad, then follow Gran's slow steps upstairs. My crutches are loud on the wooden steps, and they echo in the narrow stairwell. I'm careful to make sure each crutch is firmly planted on the step above me before climbing.

"You all right on those stairs, sweetie?" Gran asks. "They can sometimes be a bit slippery."

"I'm good, thanks." I reach the top and am finally able to look up from my feet. I hadn't noticed the skylight at the top of the stairs and at this moment, the moon is creeping into view through the glass. Directly in front of me, Gran is standing in one of the bedroom doorways.

"This was your mom's room, Meranda. It's been waiting for a child to fill it up again." She squeezes my shoulder, then crosses the room to close the curtains. The fall breeze billows the navy fabric and fills the room with a cool salty sweetness.

"Just crawl in, sweetie. We'll unpack and look around tomorrow." Gran presses her damp cheek to mine. "Now my heart is complete. You're home, and it feels right. I love you." She leaves the door open a crack on her way out.

When McKenzie was found on the shore, he was semi-conscious. He was suffering from hypothermia and severe dehydration. His skin was blistered from the sun and heat, and he was covered in bruises and scrapes. Notes from the doctors who treated him indicate that he did not have as much water on the lungs as typically seen in cases of near-drowning. While his physical injuries may have been minimal, his mental state was in keeping with one who has suffered the extreme conditions and severe trauma associated with a shipwreck. He was described by doctors as delirious, ranting about the mermaids he claimed had carried him safely to shore inland. While experts felt his delusions were a direct result of the near-death experience, they could offer no explanation for how he had survived the ordeal relatively unharmed.

Legends of the Lakes **by Sarah Chapman, 2010**

Chapter 5

Before I open my eyes, I hear the most beautiful sound. Water. The sound of the waves splashing on nearby rocks weaves its way through the bird songs and trees rustling like a breeze on my face. For a second, I forget where I am, then I open my eyes. The unfamiliar space is blurry. I rub my eyes and reach for my glasses on the bedside table. The curtains are still drawn, but flecks of sunlight sparkle through the fabric, leaving a starry pattern on the quilt on my bed. Above me, a mobile swings in the morning breeze. Silhouettes of mermaids ascend to the ceiling and plunge down through the air. Hanging from invisible threads, they silently swim in spirals like dreams circling my head.

I prop myself up on my elbows and look around Mom's old room. The white metal bed frame squeaks with my movement. Not surprisingly, the shelves are filled with books. I get my love of reading from Mom. Sitting up I can make out the titles on some of the less battered spines: the Anne of Green Gables, Nancy Drew, and Narnia series to name a few. The bookshelf is laced with dozens of seashells and rocks tucked between the books like they're sheltered in a coral reef.

The lamp on the delicate bedside table has a white ceramic fish tail for a base and beside it is a photo in a pale blue ceramic frame. It's Mom and Grampa. She must be about my age, maybe a bit younger. They're in a green canoe on the water, and they have their heads thrown back, laughing like they've just heard the greatest joke in the world. There is a flash of light at the base of Mom's neck, like a reflected drop of sunshine. On the dresser across from me are more framed photos, and I move to the edge of the bed to have a closer look. My mother's smooth, smiling face, relaxed and happy on or in the water—fishing with Uncle Mark, jumping off a dock into the lake while other kids look on, grinning.

This girl in the pictures is a complete stranger to me. An echo of someone I thought I knew better than anyone. It's impossible to imagine Mom here, surrounded by relics and memories from the sea, in her room by the lake. And when I do, resentment rises in my throat. She had this life by the water—active, free, fun—that I can't have. I wish that I could have known the girl in these photos. Before me and my legs made her so afraid and neurotic.

The shiny flash is in all the photos, but I can't make out exactly what it is.

My thoughts are interrupted by voices.

"Beth, wait!" It's Gran's voice. She's pleading with my mother.

"I can't believe this. You lied to me. About *this*? How could you let me bring her here?" Mom's yelling, shrieking. The fury in her voice sends a shot of panic through my chest.

A chair scrapes the floor, and a door slams.

I get out of bed and remember I'm still in my clothes from yesterday. I pull my sweatshirt over my head, then lean on the footboard and then the desk to get to the window. When I pull back the curtains, I see Mom running across the yard. I turn to get my crutches and find myself at eye-level with a framed photo hanging on the wall beside the window. Mom and Gran and Grampa. Mom is wearing a cap and gown, a beaming smile on her glowing face. In this one I can make it out—a gold necklace on Mom's neck. The circular pendant has what looks like a fish tail curled inside. I've never seen Mom wear it, I'm sure of it, but still it's familiar somehow.

"Good morning, sweetheart," Gran says, appearing in the doorway. "Hungry?"

I steal a quick glance out the window. Mom is gone.

"Starving!" I answer Gran, then follow her downstairs.

"She'll be all right," Gran tells me, reading my thoughts. "She's pretty broken up about Uncle Mark, and she's exhausted."

She takes my crutches from me so I can navigate the turn on the landing of the staircase, then hands them back once my feet are on firm floor. I follow her to the kitchen.

"Have a seat, and I'll whip you up some of my world-famous scrambled eggs."

"Where is everyone?" I ask.

"Your dad went for a run, and Grampa went into town for a few things. I expect they'll both be back shortly." Her back is to me as she stirs the eggs on the stove.

I drum my fingers and flip through the papers on the counter, my stomach grumbling. A headline on the second page of the *Skye Gazette* leaps out at me: "Death of Local Man Being Investigated as Suspicious." Below the headline is a black-and-white photo of Uncle Mark on his fishing boat.

"Gran ...?" I start, but she has already turned around and is reaching for the newspaper.

"Oh! Meranda, you didn't need to see that."

"What does it mean? I thought Uncle Mark had a heart attack."

Gran looks at her feet, then up at me. She takes a deep breath and pulls out the stool beside me to sit down. "It seems they're not sure what actually happened. It's sounding now like he may have fallen overboard somehow."

"But it says 'suspicious.' How is falling overboard suspicious?"

The back door slams, and Mom enters the kitchen.

"Good morning, sweetie. How did you sleep?" Mom's face is blotchy, and her eyes are puffy, but she's trying to smile through it and act like everything's normal. So I do the same. She puts an arm around me and kisses the top of my head. "What are you guys up to?"

Then she sees the newspaper. Gran speaks before Mom can.

"She saw the paper, Beth. I'm sorry. I was telling her that now there's some thought that Mark may have fallen overboard."

Mom won't look at Gran. Why is she so angry?

"I still don't get what's suspicious about that," I insist. "Unless someone pushed him?"

"Don't be ridiculous, Meranda. Everyone loved Mark. No one would have ever tried to hurt him." Mom clearly does not want to talk about this. Her jaw is clenched, and her voice sounds strange, like she's partly holding her breath.

Gran wipes tears from her cheek with the hem of her apron. She seems to know better than to try to talk to Mom right now. She stays quiet.

“But don’t you want to know what really happened? Especially if someone killed him?” I can’t believe they could let this go.

“Please, Meranda. I just can’t,” Mom says.

“Oh! The eggs!” Gran grabs the pan off the stove.

So the three of us sit at the counter eating burned scrambled eggs and don’t talk about the fact that Uncle Mark may have been murdered.

Chapter 6

"I know what you heard and read this morning must have been pretty upsetting," Gran is saying. "It's important that you try not to worry yourself too much about it. Your mother is tired and emotional. We all are. Leave the worrying to us grown-ups, all right, love?" Gran puts her arm around my shoulder as we drive into town. She said she needed my help choosing sweets to order from the bakery for after the funeral. I know she was tasked with getting me out of the house. To give Mom some time to collect herself. I also know that Gran would normally walk to town for this but is driving because she doesn't think I can do it. I for sure could, and I would have preferred being outside, but I don't want to rock the boat. So here I sit, being treated like a little kid that they need to get out of the way for a while.

We pull into a parking spot on the side of the street in front of Kettle O' Fish Bakery and Café. The breeze that hits me when I open my door and get out of the car swirls with salty dampness and fresh bread. Like salted caramel.

"Yum," I say, closing the car door.

"Heavenly, right?" Gran smiles. "I thought we'd take a quick detour first." She points across the street. My mood improves a little more when I see where she's pointing.

"Is that the one with the mermaid scales?" I ask.

She winks at me, takes my arm, and leads me toward Mermaid Tales Gift Shop. "Your time here can't be all gloom and sadness, right? I want you to have a few happy memories of this place." She sighs and looks far away. "Mark always hoped you'd all be back one day." She says this with a smile that drops from her face when we get to the door.

"Oh my," she gasps.

There is a pile of shattered glass on the step, like it has been swept but not cleared yet, and the bottom half of the glass door has been replaced with several pieces of cardboard duct-taped together to fill the space. The tail-shaped door handle is dented and swinging from the upper part of the door frame, which is still intact. It looks like the pendulum of Gran's clock, reflecting the morning sun.

"What on earth …?"

We step inside, Gran helping me dodge the glass shards. The

shop smells like the saltwater taffy candies that Grampa always has in his pockets and hands out when he doesn't think Gran is watching. There are shelves from floor to ceiling along all the walls and racks of trinkets filling up the space in the center.

"You have a peek around. I'm going to see if I can find Colleen, the owner." Gran disappears into the store.

I move through the racks a bit like a fish darting in and out of openings in a coral reef, stopping every few seconds to look a little closer at the treasures all around me. There are mermaid keychains, postcards, T-shirts, aprons, and plush blankets that you can slip on like a mermaid tail. Toward the back is a table with lots of colorful crystal rocks, sparkling in the sunlight from the window. The rocks are propping up copies of *Legends of the Lakes* as well as a few kids' books with smiling mermaids on the covers.

"I'm sorry, Colleen. People can be so awful." I follow Gran's voice to the back of the store where she is standing at the cash with a middle-aged woman in a pink cable-knit sweater. They don't see me.

"Never had to close down for the season before Thanksgiving," the woman says. Her hands are on her hips. "Never. But I'm not sure what else to do. To tell you the truth, I'm afraid."

"Come on now," Gran says unconvincingly.

"Seriously, Gwenn. No predicting what folks will do when

they're scared. And this shop is not exactly the safest place right now with all that fear swirling out there."

I shift my weight, and the edge of my crutch bumps the rack beside me. The women stop talking and turn to look at me.

"Meranda," says the woman in the sweater, walking toward me. She puts her hands on my shoulders and kisses my cheek. She smells flowery, like the dried lavender pouches Mom puts in the drawers and closets in our cabin to prevent the musty smell. I try not to pull away. I don't want to be rude, but the unexpected affection from a stranger makes me stiffen.

"Meranda, this is Colleen. She owns the shop," Gran says, "and she's the artist of the painting in your room."

"I feel like I've known you forever," Colleen says, moving back behind the cash register. "Gwenn keeps us all up to date; you're her favorite subject. She's so been looking forward to you coming. Despite the circumstances." She lowers her voice, closes her eyes, and shakes her head.

"Uh, nice to meet you," I manage to squeak out.

Thankfully, Gran jumps in. "Meranda's hoping to see the mermaid scales, Colleen."

"Of course," Colleen says, waving us to the other side of the shop, by the window. The light on the floor is marbled with reds, blues, and purples, and when I look up, I see why. The window is mostly covered with thin, flat, baseball-sized glass circles of every color hanging from invisible threads. "Here they are. Pretty, eh?" She runs her hand through the scales, watching the colors dance on the floor. But I can tell from her expression she's worried.

I pick out a blue scale to bring home. We pay, say goodbye to Colleen, who hugs me again (which doesn't feel quite as weird as the first time), and leave the shop.

"Are people afraid because of what happened to Uncle Mark?" I ask Gran. We're walking back toward the bakery where we parked the car. "Is it because he was killed? Is there a murderer out there?"

I can't read Gran's expression at all. She's thinking of what to say to me. "Of course not," she sighs. "You have to understand, this is a small town. It's a little bit like a big dysfunctional family—with a very superstitious history. People cope with tragedy and loss in their own ways … and fear spreads fast."

Fear? Of what? It had to be about what I saw in the paper—that maybe there's a murderer out there. I wouldn't put it past my family to hide that from me. To protect me from anything scary, like they always do. After all, I couldn't possibly be strong enough to handle this. But my frustration is tempered by another lingering question. What does Uncle Mark's murder have to do with Colleen and her shop? I look up and down the street, watching strangers going about their day, running errands. The sun ducks behind a cloud, casting shadows on the scene, revealing a darkness I didn't notice before. A darkness that gives me chills.

Chapter 7

When the bells on the door of Kettle O' Fish Bakery and Café announce our entrance, the clanking of cutlery on plates and ripples of laughter and conversations come to a halt. I feel a dozen sets of eyes looking me up and down, and when Gran walks in behind me, the eyes fall back awkwardly to plates or laps. The space is larger than it looks from the street. The light blue walls are bare, and there are at least ten square tables all placed a little too close together. Each has a tiny vase with (clearly) plastic flowers in it and a metal napkin dispenser.

"Mornin' to ya," Gran says into the room with a cheerfulness I'm sure took some effort. The uncomfortable near-silence is broken by the woman behind the counter. "Gwenn. Oh, Gwenn, I'm so sorry. Mark was one of my best customers. And one of the nicest too." She comes around from behind the till and grasps both of Gran's hands in hers. "What a tragedy. What a senseless loss. I keep prayin' that this town's luck will soon turn around."

"Thanks, Beatrice," Gran answers. "Can't quite imagine life without him. Died doin' what he loved, though, I'll give him that. He always knew it was a risky job."

Gran and Beatrice continue to talk but my attention is drawn to the display case of baked goods. One whole case is a rainbow of tarts with fillings in so many colors, I don't think I can come up with flavors to match. Then another case is stocked with squares, brownies, and cookies, and a third with homemade doughnuts and éclairs. It's not quite lunchtime yet, but I swear I could eat all of them.

"Wasn't an accident, y'know." A gruff voice tears my eyes away from a chocolate éclair. An old man has come up behind me, and when I turn, he is standing a little too close. His leathery, whiskery face and baggy wool clothes remind me of old fishermen on postcards that Gran would send me "to send a little kiss in the mail."

Once he has my attention, he says it again. "Mark McKenzie. No accident. Plain as day."

I look around for Gran. She must have ducked into the back of the shop with Beatrice. I'm on my own here. The man continues, this time putting his hand on my arm.

"But don't be goin' expecting the grand ol' Skye branch of the

RCMP to do anything about it, not that they even could. Gonna be up to us seamen in the end."

"What?" I can't help but feel I'm betraying Mom and Gran by asking about Uncle Mark's death. But I don't know how to ignore this man who is blocking my path. I want to pull my arm away without causing a scene, so I wiggle it out of his grasp and raise it to my face to tuck a stray piece of hair behind my ear. But he grabs my shoulder. This time, his claw-like fingers pull me toward him.

"They're all cowards," he whispers, his breath hot on my cheek. He gestures behind him at no one in particular. "Afraid to say it out loud, but they know it all the same."

"Know what?" I ask, following his waving arms, trying to will Gran to appear.

"Mermaids." His voice gets quieter. "Vicious and bloodthirsty monsters." He raises his eyes to mine to make sure I heard him.

"Sandy, leave the poor girl alone." A woman gets up from one of the tables and puts her arm around his shoulders. He looks like a small child, being led away. His agitated expression has wilted to bewilderment.

"It's all right," I say, gulping down my unease, trying to look braver than I feel. It seems cruel for this shrinking man to be scolded.

"Don't mind Sandy, dear. He's spent one too many nights on the water, this one. Has a head full of stories, right, Sandy?" The woman laughs kindly. "Don't you go trying to fill this girl's head with cartoon conspiracies now."

"But"—Sandy tries to wiggle out of her kind grip—"they're all in on it. Cover-up. Cover-up, I tell ye."

"Where's your tea now, anyway?" she says, then sits him down at one of the square tables in the center of the room, sliding a teacup into his hands. He blinks and accepts it, taking a long sip of the steaming drink. "See? All better now." She meets my gaze and tilts her head toward Sandy in pity.

I smile back politely. Mermaids? In real life? Now that's a break from reality. That poor man.

Gran must have heard the commotion. She rushes out of the kitchen, wiping fresh tears from her face.

"Meranda? You all right?" Her red eyes dart around the tiny room.

"I told ye! Cover-up!" Sandy is shouting and pointing at me from his table. He is trying to stand up, but the woman beside him has her hands on his shoulders to keep him in his seat.

"Easy now. Sandy, please." She stands over him, blocking me from his view.

Gran puts an arm around my shoulder and pulls me toward

the door. “I think we should go. Poor ol’ Sandy’s not well, and we seem to be upsetting him.” On the sidewalk outside, she looks at me apologetically. “I’m so sorry I left you out there on your own. I lost track of the time. Bea and I were remembering Mark together. They were good friends in school. I didn’t realize I still had so many tears in here.” She pats her heart, then pulls a tissue from the inside of her sleeve to wipe her nose. “Good enough,” she says, sniffling and standing up straighter. “Better get moving.”

Gran is walking too fast, and I can’t keep up. Then she remembers and stops to wait for me. She is distracted but tries to refocus her attention on me.

“You all right, dear? I can see how that would have been a bit upsetting.”

Upsetting? Sure, that poor man had been pretty creepy at first, but *mermaids*? After that, I felt more sorry for him than afraid. But he had also mentioned a cover-up. Between Sandy, Colleen, and the newspaper headline this morning, I’m now sure that my family is hiding something from me. I clench my fists on the handles of my crutches and my chest gets tight. Why can’t they see that I’m not a baby? That I’m an actual part of this family and won’t break into a million pieces with bad news. If Uncle Mark was murdered, or they suspect foul play, and that’s what all the whispers and stares have been about, I deserve to know. I decide to say that to Gran, to demand an answer.

After she unlocks the car and holds the door open for me, she runs her hand through her graying hair and rests it on the back of her neck. Staring off down the street, blinking hard, she looks so tired, trying to contain her heartbreak. I have never seen Gran like this. The tear running down her cheek melts some of my frustration. For now.

"I can't tell you how it warms my heart to have you here, Meranda." She clasps my hand and kisses it before taking my crutches and helping me into the car. By the time she has put them in the trunk and taken her seat behind the wheel, any thoughts I had about confronting this woman have been washed away.

Chapter 8

Dad's in the kitchen when we get home.

"How about I hop in the shower real quick and then we'll head out and explore?" He has finished scarfing down the rest of Gran's eggs after his run. "We could go for a walk along the shore together if you like?"

"YES, please!"

"'Kay, back in a flash."

I open the screen door at the back of the house and curl up on a wicker couch on the deck. The sun warms my face, and I close my eyes. In the pink glow behind my eyelids, I replay the scenes at breakfast and in town. Maybe Mom and Gran are so overcome by grief and loss that they can't or won't face the truth about what happened to Uncle Mark. Or, more likely, they already know and just won't tell me. With that thought, the knot tightens in my stomach. Why won't they treat me like a true member of this family? Instead of an only child, precious and fragile, frozen in time.

"Whatcha dreaming about?" Grampa says, coming around the side of the house. "You look pretty comfy up there." He turns on the hose and starts filling up a watering can.

"Grampa, did you know that Uncle Mark's death may not have been an accident?"

He glances behind him and then inside the house through the window. "What's this now?"

"I saw the headline in the paper. And Gran and Mom don't even seem to care."

"Well now, girlie. If you'd had a chance to read the article, you'd know that this is all a load of hogwash. Folk around here are pretty superstitious and never seem satisfied with simple truths."

"What do you mean?" I ask. "What did the article say?"

"No need filling your head with nonsense. Point is, Mark is gone. Best to mourn him and then move on." Grampa turns off the hose and puts the heavy watering can down for a moment.

"That's what Mom said," I answer. "But don't you want to know the truth?"

"Sometimes the truth doesn't make you feel any better and may simply stir up things best left alone." He gets quiet then, and I am about to ask him what the heck that means when Dad comes bounding down the stairs and out the screen door.

"Ready to check out the lake, kiddo?"

Grampa has disappeared again around the side of the house, so I jump off the couch and follow Dad across the lawn.

He grabs my elbow when we get closer to the stairs at the end of the yard, and I don't mind one bit. The truth is, I'm a bit nervous heading down to the water. Mom's voice echoes in my brain—"All it takes is one misstep, and your life will never be the same again" and "It's just not worth the risk" and "Life can change in a flash." I meet Dad's eyes, and he squeezes my arm. I wonder if he's hearing the same voice. At the top of the stairs with the trees behind us, the view is incredible. The edge of the lake reaches out to rolling hills to the right and stretches out to the horizon on my left. In front of me are white cliffs that glow orange in the late morning sun.

"Is it what you thought it'd be?" Dad asks.

"I'm not sure," I answer. "I mean, I've seen lots of pictures, so I knew how it would look, but I guess it all feels bigger than I expected."

He looks confused.

"Like, I guess I feel a bit small standing here. The hills are huge even so far away and the smells are huge and my feelings are … huge. I guess I'm not sure how I feel," I say with a sheepish grin.

"Deep," says Dad as he lovingly jabs my shoulder with his.

We both laugh and descend the steps to the dock. The stairs are steep and have narrow footing, and my forearms burn with my weight on my crutches. Dad stays one step ahead and lets me take my time.

"Truth? I feel like a bit of a brat wanting to check everything out and see this place when Mom's so sad."

"I know. Just remember how much she loves you and that having you here makes everyone feel a bit better."

I take the last step, then walk out onto the dock. As it bobs in the gentle waves, I almost lose my balance. "Whoa!"

"It'll take some time to find your sea legs!" Dad and I are giggling.

"This is amazing. I love how the air even *smells* wet." My insides slosh with the movement under the dock, while my nervous laugh echoes off the cliffs and bounces back to me to remind me of my fear—or my mother's fear—of the water.

"Nothing like it in the world," Dad says with his eyes closed. "I sure have missed this. I've been landlocked for far too long."

My breathing slows, and I'm finally able to steady myself. I sit down to dip my fingers in the cool water as it laps up to kiss the edge of the dock. It's not nearly as cold as I expected, and the fear in my gut is instantly and completely washed away by the water on my hand. I feel still, like the mirrored surface of the lake, calm and comforted, like I'm coming home. My arm disappears into the dark water, and I make waves of my own that splash up onto the dock. Then, suddenly the calm surface in the center of the lake is broken by waves. They seem to be growing as they're moving, coming toward us at an alarming speed. The dock starts to sway, lurching in the choppy water.

"Meranda! Get away from the edge NOW! GO!" Dad grabs my arm, pulls me to my feet, and practically carries me up the stairs.

"What *was* that?" I say once I can find my breath. We're standing halfway up the stairs from the dock, and Dad is clutching me in his arms so tightly I can feel his heart racing in his chest.

He sets his jaw, his eyes focused on the water. "Weather sure can change quickly here," he says. "It's a good reminder of the dangers of this lake."

I frown. Are you kidding me? I can't say this out loud, of course, but come on. The water was calm, then it wasn't. Calm, then a killer wave front heading our way? Seriously?

"I can't believe how quickly the wind picked up there." Dad

lets me go and checks me from head to toe. "Quite the gust."

"I didn't notice any wind," I say.

"That's open water for you," he answers. "Weather patterns change before you even notice."

With that, we're back in the yard and approaching the house. I have to stop for a minute. My legs are throbbing. I lean on Dad and stretch them out as best I can, bending over to massage my calves one at a time.

"Okay?" he asks, looking worried again.

"Yeah," I answer. "I guess my legs aren't used to sprinting up rickety wooden stairs to escape lake tsunamis." Even though that's true, what I don't say is they've felt heavier and more painful since getting off the plane. I hope it'll pass.

Dad winces. "Probably best not to tell Mom about this," he says sheepishly. "She's got lots going on in her head right now and doesn't need to add the image of you nearly drowning in the lake to the list." He winks at me, and I can't resist a smile. "And there's a chance I'd get in trouble for even bringing you down here this morning."

"Sure thing, Dad." I want to ask him more. He is clearly rattled by what happened and is spitting out excuses and silly explanations as quickly as he can. I think he's trying not to give me any time to think about what he has told me. But that's not going to happen. Was it an animal? Or … a mermaid? As if. Maybe there are whales that find their way through the channel into the lake. Or seals. But why wouldn't Dad just say that? I'm about to ask him when I notice Grampa standing on the deck. I wonder if he saw us bolting up the stairs.

"Crazy gust of wind out there," Dad says and slides one of the chairs over next to Grampa's. "Big waves! Almost thrown from the dock this time!"

Grampa raises his eyebrows and mutters under his breath, "*Dìon maighdeann-mhara … dìon maighdeann-mhara*." He shakes his head sadly.

On June 3, 1973, Laura Fraser and her infant son, John, were enjoying a sunny afternoon on the dock by their home off Campbell Road. The water was calm and the four-month-old was playing on a blanket when the unthinkable happened. His mother recalled the near-tragedy in a statement to the Skye Gazette—*"He was cooing and giggling on his blanket on the dock. I was right there with him. Then our dog, Skipper, started barking like mad and running all over. Must've seen something in the water.*

"Before I knew what had happened, he'd knocked John right into the water. I ran to the edge, terrified. I don't swim, you see. And my John was just floatin' there, looking at me. Like he was being lifted up from underneath. I reached down and scooped him up, then there was a mighty splash, like a giant tail slapping the surface." John was taken to Skye Regional Medical Centre where he was examined and given a clean bill of health. Doctors told the family that it was a miracle for a small infant to survive such an event with no signs of harm. Was it a miracle? Laura Fraser doesn't think so. She credited mermaids for saving her boy. "They held him up, protected him. Dìon maighdeann-mhara."

Legends of the Lakes **by Sarah Chapman, 2010**

Chapter 9

When I go back into the house, I find Gran and Mom sitting at the dining room table working on Gran's laptop.

"Hi, sweetie," Mom says as I pull up a chair beside her. "We're working on the eulogy."

"I can't seem to find the right words on my own," Gran says. "I don't know how to say goodbye to my little brother."

"We'll get it right," Mom says. She rubs Gran's arm. "We'll work on it some more when we get back."

"Back from where?" I ask.

"I've got an appointment with Reverend Tim at the church to review final arrangements for the funeral. We won't be long. Dad and Grampa are heading over to help John from next door with his boat, but they shouldn't be too long either." Gran is getting up and searching for her purse. She finds it and tucks it under her arm.

"Can I come?" I ask. I'm hoping to see a bit more of the town before everyone gets even busier with the funeral. And if I'm honest, I'm a bit afraid of being here alone after what just happened on the dock.

Before Mom and Gran can exchange glances, I add, "Pleeeeeease?"

"Sure, sweetheart. I'm so glad to have you here, I won't argue with having you right close." Gran kisses the top of my head and grabs her keys.

I look over at Mom. She smiles at me and says, "Maybe bring a book or something so you don't get too bored."

I grab the copy of *Anne of Avonlea* I snagged from Mom's old bookshelf and head out the door with them.

The church is right in the heart of town. As we drive, Mom comments on how everything has changed. "What happened to the McDonnell's place? It's a mess. What a shame. When did the clinic close? Did old Mr. Cameron retire yet?" Then she gets quiet for a while and stares out the window.

I see the church's black-and-white steeple poking through the trees in front of us before we reach the building itself. Then a small structure with white siding and black trim comes into view as we pull off the main road. The church is nestled between two sections of forest with a clearing behind it. I didn't really notice that we'd driven up so high since we'd been surrounded by trees the whole time, but suddenly I see we're way above the lake. The light reflects off the water and into the church, lighting the stained-glass windows so it looks like the building is glowing from the inside out.

A man comes out to greet us when we get out of the car. Dressed in jeans and an old cable-knit sweater, he doesn't look the part of a pastor, but Gran says, "Hi, Reverend. Thanks for meeting us."

"Of course, Gwenn, you're most welcome." He turns to Mom and offers his hand. "Beth? It's good to see you. It's been a long time. We're all so sorry about Mark. He was a good man."

"Thanks, Reverend. It's good to be home again. This is my daughter, Meranda." She puts her arm loosely around my shoulders when she introduces me.

"It's her first time back to the island," Gran says.

"Is it now?" He seems surprised. "Welcome. Now, let's get started so you can move on to taking Meranda down memory lane."

I spot a stone bench near the edge of the trees between the clifftop and the cemetery. "Can I sit out here with my book while you guys go inside?"

Mom looks toward the cliff edge and hesitates for a split

second. "Good idea. It's such a gorgeous day." Then she can't resist: "Just stay away from the edge."

I make my way toward the bench by way of the cemetery. Dozens of white headstones are arranged in neat rows. The grass around them has been recently mowed, and I can smell the sweetness of the cuttings as I wander between the graves. I notice familiar names from my grandparents' stories, with dates that are decades and centuries old. Generations of Cape Bretoners whose families are still settled nearby. Many of the stones have ships or ocean designs carved above the names—these people made their livelihood on the waves and died there too. Fishermen, sailors, fathers, uncles. I imagine Uncle Mark on the boat he loved so much. I wonder what could have happened to knock, or push, him overboard. I think of him struggling beneath the waves with his crew scrambling on deck to try to save him.

"Can I help you find someone?" My thoughts are interrupted by a gravelly voice. I turn around and see a man pushing a wheelbarrow along the edge of the cemetery. His face is obscured by the stained blue cap he's wearing, but I judge from the way his body is moving with slow persistence that he must be ancient. His pants have dirt stains on the knees and his plaid wool shirt is rolled up at the sleeves.

"Uh, no. Just looking, thanks," I stammer as if I'm browsing in a store.

He approaches, stooping occasionally to brush a branch off a headstone or pick a weed out of the grass. When he looks up, closer now, I'm surprised at how young his eyes are. He must be around Gran's age, but his body moves like it has lived a whole other lifetime without him.

"Some of 'em are quite beautiful, aren't they?" He gestures toward a stone that's facing the water. "This is one of my favorites."

I walk toward him to get a look at the front. Carved into the white marble is the silhouette of a mermaid with curls trailing behind her head and delicate fins billowing from the end of her tail. Under the image is the name "James McDermitt" and the dates "1910–1991." The inscription reads "Back to the sea at last." I look up to see the man watching me intently. The stone behind him also has a mermaid image carved into it, but this one holds a small child above her head. It reads "Laura Fraser 1949–2006 *dìon maighdeann-mhara—Forever Grateful.*" I know that name. From my *Legends* book, the one who believed her baby was saved by mermaids.

"Not from 'round here, then?" the man asks.

"Visiting family," I reply. "Funeral."

"Mark McKenzie?"

"He was my great-uncle. How'd you know?" I ask.

"Small town," he says, "and folk around here take note of these kind of incidents. Fuels the fear. Name's Duncan, by the way. Alex Duncan."

I frown, taking in what he said. "What do you mean 'fuels the fear'?"

"'Bout the merfolk. Y'know, bein' out to get us. Nonsense if you ask me. Some bad things are accidents, plain and simple."

"Is that what the newspaper meant by Uncle Mark's death being 'suspicious'? Mermaids?" I can't quite believe those words just escaped my lips.

"You think that sounds crazy, do ya? So do I. They've been our protectors for centuries. I won't believe that they've been the cause of all the pain and mischief these past years. There's no denying this town has been plagued by bad luck at sea lately, but there's lots of reasons that could be. Take that global warming for instance … and maybe our selkie protectors have moved on or died off, but surely they're not out to hurt us."

"Selkie?" I ask, already knowing the answer.

"Merfolk."

I reach out to touch the stone mermaid, running my fingers over the intricate stone scales, warmed by the autumn sun.

A gasp. Alex is looking at my arm. My birthmark. The color has drained from his stubbled cheeks. He staggers backward, away from me. "Miracle Baby," he whispers.

"Are you all right, Mr. Duncan?" I offer my arm to help steady him, but he recoils as if he's been struck.

"I … uh … it's just that I … I … best be goin'." He turns and stumbles back toward the church.

I hear the beep of our car doors being unlocked. Mom and Gran are saying goodbye to Reverend Tim. Mom calls out, "Meranda, let's go."

I plant my crutches in the soft grass and walk toward the parking lot. I'm almost at the car when I notice Alex leaning against the doorframe at the back of the church. He covers his mouth with his hand so all I can see are his eyes, wide with terror, staring at me.

Chapter 10

"Who were you talking to out there?" Mom asks as we drive away from the church. I haven't been able to speak since we got in the car

"Alex … Duncan, I think he said his name was …? I think he works in the cemetery. He got totally freaked out by—"

"Yep," interrupts Gran, "caretaker, groundskeeper, historian, Jack-of-all-trades-type. I went to school with his sister, Nancy. Nice family. Alex takes such good care of that church. The yard always looks perfect. Shall we grab some lunch in town before heading home? Meranda, we have to take you to the Chowder House. I know you've been hearing about it your whole life! You'll love it, and I think we can all use some comfort food, right, Beth?"

"Sure, Mom. Sounds good."

The Chowder House is a family legend. Grampa proposed

to Gran there, it was Mom's favorite place to eat growing up, and Mom and Dad say they've never had seafood chowder as good anywhere. Not even close. Anytime Dad orders chowder anywhere, he pretends he's hopeful, then after one bite declares it a grim failure. Every time. I'm happy to finally get to go there—but it doesn't distract me from my nagging question.

"So something weird happened at the cemetery." I tell them about Alex and his strange comments. "It was like the guy at the bakery."

Mom and Gran exchange glances in the front seat.

"Guy at the bakery?" Mom asks.

"Yeah, this poor old man grabbed me and went on about—"

Gran interrupts. Again. "Beth, it was nothing. Old Sandy McLean, talking legends and folklore. And as for Alex Duncan, I'm afraid he too has his share of troubles." Gran is looking at me in the rearview mirror. "Poor Alex used to be a seaman too. He's seen his fair share of maritime tragedy, I'm sad to say. Nancy tells me that his memories get triggered sometimes working in that cemetery. Like flashbacks, she says. He's known lots of the people buried there. I suppose it's a bit like that post-traumatic stress we hear about these days. We never used to have a word for it."

"But it was *me* that triggered him," I tell them. "My birthmark, I think."

“I’m sure that wasn’t it, sweetie.” Gran looks over her shoulder at me, taking her eyes off the road for a second, then glances at Mom. “Now then. Here we are.”

Clearly that line of discussion is over. I give in. For now.

Gran parks in front of a tiny yellow cottage overlooking the lake. When I open my door, the car fills with the most wonderful smell. “Can you smell the biscuits?” Mom asks. “Nothing can ever compare to this.”

Inside, the smell is intensified by the warmth from the kitchen. It’s so humid that some of the windows are steamy, and the restaurant hums with voices and activity. The tiny place is covered with nautical artifacts. The back wall is draped with a huge fishing net laced with seashells, buoys, and plastic shellfish, and along the side wall, the windows are round, like portholes. Fiddle music fills the room from a small speaker by the front entrance. With the décor and the buzz of people in the small space, I feel like we’ve walked into an aquarium. There’s even a treasure chest in the back corner that I half expect to open and close, letting bubbles escape into the air.

We sit in a booth by a window at the back of the dining room. I’m momentarily distracted by the spectacular view of the hills surrounding the lake. The whitecaps of the waves dot the dark surface of the water, and there are spots of yellow and red in the forest along the edge of the shore, a reminder that summer is fading.

Mom takes my hand, pulling it away from my arm. "You'll rub it raw," she says. I was rubbing my birthmark again. She shifts in her seat and hands me a leaflet. "It's the program for the funeral service," she says. On the front is a photo of Uncle Mark. I turn it over to see the obituary on the back.

"They spelled my name wrong," I point out, "as usual." Meranda is usually spelled with an "i," not an "e." *Mir*anda, not *Mer*anda. My parents were clearly not thinking when they filled out my birth certificate. Mom says they thought the variation in the spelling would make it unique. But this *unique* spelling has added an extra step for me to every first day of school, every sign-up sheet, birthday invitation, you name it. I've often wondered if it was a typo, and my parents just won't admit it.

The picture of Uncle Mark on the front makes me smile. He's on a boat, leaning on the front part—bow or stern, I can never remember—like he's looking out to sea. His face is leathery and tanned, but I see Gran in his eyes. There's something else. The symbol on the chain around his neck. I've seen it before. It looks like the one Mom was wearing in the old photos in her room.

"Beth Campbell? Is that you?" A shriek from the kitchen precedes a short blond woman with a bright yellow apron charging toward our table. "I wondered if you'd be back. So sorry about Mark. When did you get here? How long are you staying? We'll have to catch up. It's been so long. I—" She pauses, her face strained.

"Whoa, Kel. Slow down. Good to see you too. And it's Morgan now." Mom's voice sounds strange, forced. "This is my daughter, Meranda. Meranda, meet Kelly McLean. Kel and I have been friends since kindergarten."

"Until you up and disappeared without a word!" Kelly offers her hand, and I shake it. "Nice to meet you, Meranda." She glances over at Gran. "Your grandmother talks so much about you that I'm sure the whole island knows what you ate for breakfast!" She laughs with an awkwardly high-pitched squeal. "Welcome to Skye. You must be about ten now?" Her eyes narrow a bit as she counts on her fingers. "You've pretty much been gone what, seven years, Beth?"

"I'm eleven," I say. "Just."

"Ah, eight years gone then." I sense some bitterness in her voice, but her smile is unwavering. Then she tilts her head, studying my face. "Doesn't much look like either of you, eh, Beth?"

I feel Mom's body tense next to me, the vinyl surface of the bench squeaking subtly under her legs. But I'm used to this. Next to my red-headed mom and blond dad, I often get confused looks.

"Inheritance is a funny thing," Dad said to me once when I was little, after some mean kid at school tried to convince me I was adopted. "Genes turn on and off and cancel each other out in unpredictable ways. Like grains of sand being tossed in the waves, before landing on a random shore. Biology is beautiful." He touched a strand of my dark hair before kissing my forehead. "Like you."

"Let me bring y'all some chowder, and we'll find time to catch up later." And with that, Kelly dashes back into the kitchen.

"Looks like Kel hasn't changed much." Mom unfolds her napkin and looks over at me. "I'm not so good at keeping in touch."

We sit together swirling in our own thoughts, Mom picking at her cuticles. The mermaid cartoon on the paper placemat in front of me is suddenly not as cartoonish as it would have been an hour ago.

Kelly mercifully brings steaming bowls of chowder to the table with a basket of the famous biscuits. The warm food has a calming effect on all of us. The mood lightens, and I watch the lines on Mom's face fade for a while. And Dad is right. I have never tasted anything so good.

When we're finished, I make a quick stop in the washroom before meeting Gran and Mom at the car. On my way out, walking toward the door of the restaurant, I hear Kelly's voice from the kitchen. I'm not sure who she's talking to, but her voice is shrill and loud.

"Disappears without a word, like she fell off the face of the earth! And then comes back, with her *miracle* baby, without so much as an email? Like none of the rest of us were hurting too? Ditched us all. After how this town rallied around her? And now today, she couldn't seem to get out of here fast enough, y'know? Just burns me up." The last sentence trails off, then the kitchen door swings open, and Kelly comes out with a tray full of steaming bowls. I turn my back to her, wait for her to pass, then go out the front door to the parking lot. What was Kelly talking about? Mom and Dad moved away for Mom's new job in Calgary, they didn't *disappear*. And she's now the second person to call me a "miracle baby." Mom sure seemed uncomfortable being called out by this woman at the table, but I assumed that was her feeling guilty for not keeping in touch. There's more to this, I'm sure of it.

"One quick stop, then home, okay?" Gran says when I get into the car. "Got a package to pick up."

As we approach the post office a few minutes later, I see

flashing lights. A woman in uniform stands beside a police car in the parking lot.

"I wonder what this is all about," says Gran.

"Looks like we're about to find out," Mom says, tension in her voice.

Gran parks the car in the tiny dirt lot, and we all get out. Immediately, it's clear what's wrong: there's a statue lying on the ground beside the post office sign. It's a mermaid. The arms are broken off, which probably happened when the statue fell over, and there are paint splashes across the front of the body. The police officer is standing over it, scribbling in a notebook.

"Hi, Molly," Gran says to the officer. "What's all this?"

"Oh, hey, Gwenn. More vandalism, I'm afraid. Happens with every incident now. Mark was the first death in a while, though, so I expect this isn't the end of folk lashing out."

Incident? I practically scream inside my head. Waves of questions pound me from the inside. And there have been others? Caused by whom … mermaids? No. People angry at mermaids? I hold my breath to keep my thoughts from spilling out into the open silence. Am I seriously in a place where I'm wondering about violent mermaids? Like a topsy-turvy world where legends and fairy-tale creatures come to life? What's next—singing forest animals, magic carpets, fiery dragons?

"I had no idea things were getting so bad," Gran says under her breath. She glances nervously at Mom, who grabs my arm and practically drags me back to the car.

As we pull out onto the road, I can tell by the looks on Mom's and Gran's faces that I should keep my mouth shut for now and do as I'm told. So I do. For now.

Sandy McLean, an avid bird-watcher, was out enjoying the early summer fauna just after sunrise on June 23, 1989. He stopped to make a pot of tea on his camp stove at his favourite spot overlooking Skye Harbour when he noticed an unusual shape on the water's surface below. Wondering if it could be a small whale or a piece of driftwood, he set up his scope to investigate further.

McLean remembers, "It was plain as day. It was a man. A man somehow standing smack in the middle of the lake. Impossible, I know. I didn't believe it either." When he realized what he may have been looking at, McLean set up his camera to take a picture. The resulting photo shows a dark shadow interrupting the sun's reflection on the lake. Behind the shadow, the sun is rising and has almost crested above the horizon. The shadowy figure has a human outline, with a head and shoulders above a narrow torso that disappears below the glistening water. Experts state the shadow could be a result of unusual reflection and refraction of light on the water or perhaps a small whale breaching. McLean, however, is sure he knows what it was. "I know what I saw. 'Twas a merman. No doubt."

Legends of the Lakes **by Sarah Chapman, 2010**

Chapter 11

I hear Grampa and Dad chatting loudly as we climb the porch steps to the front door. When they meet us in the hall, their conversation grinds to a halt and they don somber faces. If I wasn't so freaked out by what just happened, I would have found the exchange of "knowing looks" between the adults in my family pretty funny. Gran to Grampa, Dad to Mom, Mom to Grampa and back to Gran, Grampa to Dad, then they all converge on me for a fraction of a second before all eyes dart away as if they've been caught sharing a secret.

A swell of frustration meets a ripple of fear inside me. I'm struck with impatient courage. Enough.

"All right. When is someone going to tell me what is going on?" I ask, meeting everyone's gaze one at a time. "Anyone? Or does this 'miracle baby' have to figure it out on her own?"

That last bit does it. No one seems to know what to do. The

eye-darting then converges on Mom.

"Okay, honey. You're right." She sighs and reaches out to pat my arm. "You deserve as much of an explanation as we can give you. How about we head outside to the gazebo and talk?"

"Great idea," says Grampa. "But first let me get you both some tea."

Dad clears his throat, but Mom shoots him an "I got this" look, and he's quiet.

Gran and Grampa seem relieved, but I am suddenly not so sure I want to be let in on their secret. Maybe there is some safety in being the kid, being protected from bad things? Too late now. I can't (or won't) take back my burst of assertiveness. Mom carries our mugs, and we make our way across the yard. The blue sky has clouded over since we got home, and the gentle breeze is building like it's pushing me forward. In the semi-shelter of the gazebo, Mom settles onto the cushioned bench and puts our mugs down on the glass table in the center. She looks as nervous as I feel. I want to hug her and tell her it's okay. She doesn't need to worry about me, she doesn't need to tell me anything. I want us to feel safe and protected together. But I don't. I wait.

She pats the seat beside her. I rest my crutches up against the screen window and sit. She strokes my hair for a second, then her hand falls to her lap.

"Sometimes I forget you're not so little anymore. You're an intuitive, smart girl, and I'm sure you've noticed some strange things these last few days."

Duh. Strange is a bit of an understatement. "Maybe a little," I say instead.

"I'm sorry you've been in the dark, Meranda. I was a bit thrown by all this too. I suppose I shouldn't have been, but I guess with having been gone so long and then the shock of Uncle Mark, I … I just …" She stops and puts her palm on the screen of the window like she's reaching across the lake. "This is such a beautiful place. A magical place to grow up, to raise a family, to grow old. This was where we were supposed to be … until …"

"The job offer in Calgary?" I try to fill in the blanks.

"In a sense," Mom answers. "You see, things were changing here when the job offer came. Changing for the worse. We needed an out, so we took it."

This isn't the story. The story is, they were planning on living in Cape Breton forever, but the local hospital closed, and Mom was offered the job of a lifetime in Calgary. That's our story. Mom must see the wheels turning behind my bewildered eyes.

"Let's try this again, shall we?" She turns to face me. "This is a magical place. Some believe it is *truly* magical. You know the stories and legends, right?"

“Mermaids?” I ask cautiously, afraid this sounds ridiculous.

“Mermaids,” she answers.

What?

“Are the stories true, then?”

“I sure used to believe in them, like you did, reading that book when you were little,” Mom says. “You used to tie your socks together and pretend to swim along the hardwood floors.” She smiles, lost in a memory for a moment. “I was a little girl growing up in a small town that was said to be under the protection of mermaids. Who wouldn’t want to believe? I heard about stories of fishing vessels being guided out of storms, sightings of tails in the bays, even a baby being rescued after falling off a dock. You know the ones, from your *Legends* book. Those stories are the narrative of this place. They were the air we breathed.”

I remember the carving on the headstone at the cemetery—the child in the mermaid’s arms. “Did you ever see one?”

A flicker of hesitation, less than a heartbeat.

“No. Not exactly. But I believed that they were out there, looking out for us. That this town had an incredible secret hidden from the rest of the world. That we were special. Bound together by the protection of mermaids, *dìon maighdeann-mhara.* But then everything changed.” She takes a sip from her steaming mug and seems to disappear in her memories for a moment.

"What happened?"

"No one knows for sure. But just as we had felt the mermaids' protection, we began to feel their absence. Vessels capsized, more accidents." Again, I know this from my book, but this feels different. Like an undertow you knew was out there but didn't really believe in until it grabbed you and pulled you down.

"Uncle Mark?" I ask.

Mom gives her head a shake like she's emerging from a daydream. "Of course, the most likely explanation for all this is superstition and fear. Folks like to use legends and magic to explain things they don't understand. Or don't want to understand. Accidents happen on the water. Fishing, boating, they're dangerous, everyone knows that. Uncle Mark fell overboard. No one saw it happen, and it's easier to blame evil mermaids than it is to admit he may have made a mistake or been clumsy." There's a strange stiffness to Mom's voice, like she's reciting a script, saying the words she's supposed to say.

"Hang on," I say, trying to put this together. "We've read the *Legends* book hundreds of times. Why are you only telling me all this now?" I flash back to Mom trying to answer my mermaid questions when I was little, after Gran or Grampa had read to me at bedtime. "They're fairy tales, sweetie," she'd say. "That's what legends are."

Mom is quiet.

"Do you still believe in mermaids, Mom?"

She stares into the mug in her hands. "I had to grow up, Meranda. Your dad and I wanted a baby for so long. With you in our lives, we couldn't stay in a place like this. This whole town was unhinged, filled with such irrational fear. It wasn't a place to raise a child anymore. We moved away and have stayed away—for you."

"And what about 'miracle baby'?" I ask.

Mom inhales a quick breath like she's been kicked, then sits up straight and looks directly at me.

"Where did you hear that?"

"I overheard Kelly saying it today at the Chowder House, on my way back from the bathroom." I decide not to tell her that Alex called me that too.

"What else did she say?" Mom looks afraid.

"Just that you guys left quickly and never came back," I tell her. "She seemed … upset."

Relief crosses her face. "I don't know." Mom doesn't meet my eyes. "We had such trouble having a baby. I'd had a few early miscarriages and was utterly heartbroken after each one. Kelly was my best friend and was there through it all. And she was there when you finally arrived. My miracle." She wipes a tear from the corner of one eye before it has a chance to slide down her cheek. "You were three years old when we left. This is a small town, and everyone knew you. You captured hearts even then. We all heard at the Chowder House today how terrible I have been at keeping in touch. I know some people were angry when we left. I hurt some of my friends. A small town doesn't forget." She looks out at the water. "And with Mark … everyone is emotional."

I'm not sure that's the whole answer, but it's clear it's as much as I'm going to get for now. I wish Mom would just level with me. She's telling me some of the truth, but I can tell she is still holding something back.

"So you left Cape Breton forever and moved across the country to protect me from … evil mermaids?" Those words can't really have come out of my mouth. But they did, because Mom hugs me and answers:

"You know I'd do anything to protect you, Meranda. From anything or anyone. Even evil mermaids." She winks at me and takes another sip of tea.

Chapter 12

I lie on the bed in Mom's old room, taking advantage of some alone time before dinner. I massage my achy legs wondering if it's the salty air or the dampness that is making them act up more than usual, or the long flight yesterday. On the mobile above me, mermaids bob gently on invisible threads like they're dancing slowly in the waves. I take a deep breath and blow a gust of air at the delicate figures. The mobile swings wildly, the mermaids' bodies jerking in all directions. Violent. Angry. My gaze drifts to the window at my feet. The surface of the lake reflects the shapes of the yellow and red trees on the banks like a pane of glass. I want to run to the dock and dive in. To be a part of the stillness, to bathe in the cool, calm water. But then, I imagine a group—what is a gathering of mermaids called? A school? A pod? I'll have to look that up—of mermaids beneath the surface, scheming and plotting, preparing to attack their human neighbors on the shore.

I hear the porch door close and unfamiliar voices drift up from the hall. I almost forgot. The wake.

It's starting to get loud as I head downstairs. Dad explained the wake to me on the plane on the way over. I went to one once in Calgary when Dad's colleague's father died. It was a very serious, very quiet and formal gathering at a funeral home downtown. We had to get dressed up to "pay our respects." That meant lining up to greet the family members spread out at the front of a room decorated with pictures of the man who had died. We stood around talking in hushed voices for a few minutes, then we left and went out for Chinese food. This wake was not going to be like that. A Scottish wake is more like a party for the person who has died. There's music, memories, and most importantly, whiskey. Dad warned me it might get a bit rowdy.

When I reach the landing, Gran says, "Ahh, here she is. Everyone, this is Meranda."

A small crowd of people has gathered in the living room. No one is dressed up, no one is hushed or quiet. No one is serious. They pause their conversations and look in my direction.

"Hi," I say to no one in particular.

"Meranda, this is … uh, *was* Mark's crew. Meet Larry, Gus, Abbey, Wes, Jeffrey, and Kate." As she says each name, they wave or smile in my direction.

"Nice to meet you," I say politely.

"Mark sure talked lots 'bout you, little lady," says the tallest of the bunch. Wes, I think.

"Had your school picture taped up in the cabin," says one of the women. "We always knew what you were into."

"Loved you like you was his own, I expect." The smallest of the crew, Gus, raises a glass in my direction. "Bursting with pride."

I'm not sure what to say. My cheeks start to heat up. Thankfully, Dad comes in just in time.

"Heya, kiddo. Can you gimme a hand in the kitchen?"

"Sure, Dad."

Grampa is pouring Scotch into small glasses on a big tray, and Mom is unwrapping dishes of food some of the guests have brought. I can hear the sounds of more people arriving and waves of laughter drifting in from the living room. Dad hands me a carrot to peel and sets to work chopping more vegetables for the veggie platter. I'm grateful for a simple task right now, and I'm grateful that Dad knew that would help.

"Yikes! Aarrrgh!" Dad yelps. He rushes toward the sink and holds a bleeding finger over the drain. "Stupid, stupid."

Mom rushes through the doorway from the living room like she's Batman responding to a distress beacon in the sky. How does she do that?

She examines Dad's bleeding finger. "Oh, Gabe, that'll need a stitch or two for sure," she says. "Dad, would you grab my bag from my suitcase, please?"

Mom carries a basic medical kit wherever we go. Part of her expectation that horrible things can happen at any time, I suppose. When Grampa comes back with the kit, Mom sits down next to Dad at the kitchen table and sets to work. She's calmer than I've seen her since we left home. She's in her zone. Expertly, she threads two stitches in Dad's finger and kisses his lips before packing everything back in her kit and going upstairs to put it away.

"And that's why she's the greatest woman there is," Dad says and winks at me.

Gran comes into the kitchen with a girl about my age beside her.

"Meranda, this is Claire. She's the granddaughter of Grampa's friend Jim. Sarah and Jim have her and her brother with them for the weekend while her folks are on the mainland. I'd clean forgotten. I bet you two could use a break from all this adult company for a while."

Claire looks like I feel. Like a fish out of water. Her blue eyes dart around nervously under her red bangs, and she stuffs her hands in the pockets of her camo cargo pants. "Hi," she squeaks.

"Hey."

"Why don't you two take some food out to the gazebo and escape this crazy crowd for a while?" Gran suggests, already filling two plates for us. She hands them both to Claire so I can grab my crutches. Claire and I shrug at each other and head out back.

"So where are you from again?" Claire asks as we make our way across the lawn.

"Calgary. You?"

"Here. I'm staying at my grandparents' house while my parents are away for their anniversary. They've had it planned for months, so lucky me, now a wake and funeral become the main events of my oh-so-spectacular grandparent weekend o' fun." She rolls her eyes, then glances over at me and gasps. "OMG, I'm so sorry. You just lost your great-uncle, and I'm here acting like a spoiled jerk." She gives me a sheepish look.

I laugh at her dramatic apology. "It's all right, thanks. I didn't get to see him much. Well, not in person anyway. But he was a pretty neat guy." I realize then that I am going to really miss my time with Uncle Mark. "My mom and Gran are pretty devastated. And I've been a bit rocked by some … well, some family stuff."

"Well, sorry just the same," she says again. "I bet your family's pretty messed up about what happened, eh?" She holds the screen door of the gazebo open for me. "My grandmother says the merfolk must be super mad to have attacked a McKenzie. Says we'd all better brace ourselves, that it's us against them now." I can't read her expression.

"Huh?" I ask as we settle onto the bench.

Claire looks at me and clearly sees that I'm struggling to take in what she has just said. But who could blame me for being a bit slow? In the last few hours, I've learned many alarming things, including the fact that mermaids are maybe, sort of, potentially, real; the mermaids in the water around this town happen to be evil; my uncle may have been murdered by one of said evil merfolk; and last but not least, my parents have kept this from me my whole life.

"Of course, that's just Grandma," Claire says. "She's a bit of a local … uh … expert, I guess. On the mermaid stuff. Wrote the book. Literally."

"Literally?"

"*Legends of the Lakes*. It's a book about the mermaid legend—"

"Wait, your grandmother is Sarah Chapman? Is she in there?" I'm starstruck.

Claire rolls her eyes. "Pretty embarrassing, really."

"What do you mean?"

"Can you imagine being the kid whose grandmother is a mermaid … well … historian? I love her to bits, don't get me wrong, but I can't even count the number of times I've been called Ariel or been serenaded with 'Part of Your World.' I was two when she published the book, so it's followed me my whole life. Kids can be so mean," she says with a smirk.

I lean toward her. "So you don't believe the legends?"

"When I was little, Grandma and I used to sit on the dock and watch for mermaids. Sometimes we'd sing, hoping they'd hear our voices and join in. I can barely remember that. Grandma says the mermaids used to keep us safe. To protect us. But that something changed when I was really little. Violence. No 'sightings' in almost a decade," she says, her fingers making air quotes.

"So that's a 'no' then?" I ask, picking up on the sarcasm. Makes sense—it is pretty out-there. So then why am I starting to feel unsure?

"Seriously? Mermaids murdering people in Skye? No. I don't think so. My dad says some people will believe what they want to. Says sometimes the alternative is worse. He says Grandma has spent so long researching the myth that she's been swept away. Trouble for me is that the whole mermaid thing gets in my way sometimes."

I raise my eyebrows and wait for Claire to continue.

She swivels on the bench so she can see the lake. "After an *incident* like what happened to your uncle, the town goes a bit nutso. As much as most people around here think the mermaid stuff is a fairy-tale show for the tourists, folks still get spooked … or superstitious. Mom calls it *cautious*. For me that means lots of 'Careful near the water, Claire' or 'Don't get too close, Claire' or 'No swimming today, Claire.'"

"Oh man, can I relate to that," I say, rolling my eyes. "You have not seen cautious until you've spent a day with my mom. Reminds me of how my family gets spooked after a bear sighting at our cabin back home … I guess there's no bear spray for mermaids, huh?"

We both giggle. It feels so good to laugh that I can't stop. Our voices echo off the trees in the woods beside the house and float out over the lake, swirling with the sound of the water lapping up on the dock. The waves of laughter recede, and we sit in the stillness for a moment.

I tell Claire about the newspaper article I'd seen on the counter. "I didn't get to read it. Heaven forbid anyone around here treat me like a member of this family, but the headline said 'suspicious.' Do you think it meant mermaids? Like some of the stories in your grandmother's book?"

She wrinkles her nose. "In this place, who knows. Folks hang on to legends around here, like they're stuck in the Dark Ages."

"But if that isn't what it meant, what's the alternative?" I ask. I realize I'm gripping the chair arm super tight, almost afraid of her answer.

"Murder." The word hangs in the air. Mermaids or murder. Or murderous mermaids. "Like Dad says, sometimes the alternative is worse."

I'm not sure what to say to that. My eyes wander out over the lake. The dark water is so still, like a black mirror. Right now, it does look dangerous. Ominous.

"What's wrong with your legs?" Claire's blunt question pulls me back.

I smile at her. I'm used to this. Though most people are afraid to ask me so directly. I either hear whispered questions when people don't think I can hear them, or worse, they don't bother to ask at all. "CP," I say. She stares at me. "Cerebral palsy." She's quiet so I keep talking. "My brain has trouble controlling some of my muscles. It makes my legs stiff and weak." Claire is staring at my legs as I talk. "Lucky for me, I didn't inherit my dad's clumsiness or I'd be doomed!" I try to laugh away some of the discomfort, as I often do. But Claire seems anything but uncomfortable.

"Or maybe you're really a mermaid," she says with a laugh, "and your legs were meant to be a tail." She raises her eyebrows wryly.

"Can you imagine?" I say. "Now *that* would be a story!" I let out a snort and then we're both chuckling.

Her expression turns serious for a moment. "Is it painful?" she asks.

"My legs? Nah, not usually."

She nods. Then: "Can I try your crutches?"

And with that, any hint of awkwardness evaporates. We take turns racing around the gazebo on my crutches before collapsing into giggles on the floor.

"Last one to the dock does the dishes for the rest of the weekend!" A boy runs past the gazebo, shouting.

"As if!" Claire shouts back. But she gets up and makes her way to the steps. "My stupid brother. Coming?" She looks at me and my crutches expectantly.

"I ... uh ..." I stammer. "I'm not sure if ..." I know Mom would lose it if she saw me heading toward the dock.

"Your legs?" Claire asks.

"I'm not super strong in the water," I mumble. "I'd better stay up here." I look out and watch the boy running barefoot through the grass, the night breeze ruffling his hair. I imagine how the water would feel on my skin and long to follow. But instead, I pick up my crutches and start to make my way back toward the house, deflated.

"Wait up!" Claire grabs the dishes and runs up beside me. "Loser!" She yells over her shoulder toward the dock. "He's such a jerk sometimes. Thinks he's all that and then some. He'll chicken out when he gets down there. No way he'll go in on his own." She laughs at that.

As we get closer to the house, the porch door opens, and the night air is laced with the sound of fiddles and guitars punctuated by bursts of laughter.

"Meranda? Claire?" It's Mom. "It's getting late. Sarah and Jim are ready to head home. Come on in, please."

"Coming."

"Sean! We're going," Claire yells toward the dock. "You'd better get up here!" Then she says to me, "Grandma will skin him alive if she hears he's been down to the water."

Mom meets us halfway across the lawn. "You two seem to have hit it off. We could hear you giggling from the kitchen, and the sound did us all some good." She smiles. "I'm so glad you came tonight, Claire. Maybe the two of you can meet up again? I'm sure Meranda will want to get out of here during some of the funeral prep tomorrow."

“Sure,” we answer in unison.

At the front door, Mom and Claire’s grandmother make plans for tomorrow. Sean comes in, having cut through the back of the house. He storms past us, eyes glued to the floor, and goes out to wait in the car.

“Sorry for that,” Claire’s grandfather says to Mom and Gran. “Things have been a bit tough for these two lately.”

“Not to worry, Jim,” Gran hugs him. “Thanks for coming. Means a lot.”

“Of course, Gwenn. Gonna miss the ol’ boy.” He takes his wife’s arm and opens the door.

“Good night, Sarah. Thank you for—” Gran’s words are cut off as Claire’s grandmother abruptly closes the door behind them without a word or glance in Gran’s direction.

Chapter 13

After Claire leaves, I go back into the living room. The crowd has grown. There must be at least thirty people talking, laughing, telling stories, and drinking. In the middle of the room are three men with fiddles, two women with guitars, and an old man banging chords on Grampa's old piano in the corner. The room is tapping, drumming, buzzing.

I spot Dad on the couch across from the stairs, rubbing his bandaged finger. He grins at me, and I sit down and snuggle in beside him.

"Now this is Cape Breton," he says with a sigh. "This is my Nova Scotia."

When the song ends, Uncle Mark's crewmate Larry stands with his fiddle. The other musicians lean back and put their instruments down or their hands in their laps. The sound that comes from Larry's fiddle silences the room. He plays quietly, with his eyes closed. A mournful tune that sounds like the sea itself is weeping for a man lost. We close our eyes and let the music wash over us. There are scattered sniffles and some shifting in chairs. When the song ends, everyone silently raises their glasses in the air and bows their heads. Larry nods and bows his head too. A crewmate's beautiful goodbye.

Then, as quickly as the room fell silent, the roaring music and laughter return.

"So, big chat with Mom this afternoon?" Dad asks.

"Uh huh. She told you?"

He nods, patting my knee. "Y'know, it was really tough for her to talk about that with you. For both of us. We never planned to keep it from you for this long, but the longer we stayed away, the easier it became for us to move on and forget the past. I know she's felt pretty guilty about not telling you."

I still don't get it. What's so painful for Mom about the town deciding to blame mermaids for their bad luck? "I suppose a few things make a bit more sense now," I say, "like the irrational fear of water and the lack of trips back here."

"Old worries die hard," Dad says. "Especially for a protective mother."

I try to be generous and understanding, but the truth is, I'm not sure where to put all this in my head. Lucky for me, Dad is done talking and settles back into the music, resting his hand on top of mine. The roar of voices gradually calms to a hum as the liveliness of the occasion fades with the evening light. Conversations around the room look more serious, expressions more somber.

"What's with all the sour faces?" a voice pierces the room, words slurred. "I thought this was supposed to be a rake … a wake. The real deal." It's Mark's crewmate Gus. He stands in the middle of the living room, waving his arms. The waving throws him off balance, and he stumbles, catching himself on the edge of the coffee table to keep from falling. "Another round? Let's drink to Mark!"

"I think you've had enough toasting for tonight, Gus," Grampa takes his arm to steady him. "How be I find you a ride?"

"Nah! Me mates and I need another round. Right lads … and lasses?"

The rest of Mark's crew is sitting quietly near the back window. They look at each other, clearly deciding who will deal with Gus. Eventually, Kate gets up and puts her arm around his shoulder.

"Time to cast off, Gus," she says, rolling her eyes at her mates behind her. "I'll take you home."

Gus leans on Kate and allows himself to be led to the door. He stops to hug Gran before leaving and wipes tears from his face after pulling away. When the door closes behind them, the hum of conversation resumes.

Dad rubs my arm. "Time for bed, kiddo. I'll help you up the stairs."

I get up from the couch and lean into him as we make our way across the room, now almost empty. Through the fog of near-sleep, I swear I see flashing lights out the window at the front of the house. In a moment, they begin to fade and then disappear.

"Was that a police car?" I ask. "Why were the police here?"

I hear a sob from the kitchen and my mother's voice. She sounds almost hysterical.

"I know, Dad. I *know*. But it's more evidence that I was right. It was wrong for us to come back. How many times can I say 'I told you so'—after Steven, after Meranda, and now Mark? I will never understand how you guys can stay here."

I hear mumbled sounds in a comforting tone from Grampa. As we walk by the doorway to the kitchen, I see Mom sitting on a stool at the counter with her face buried in Grampa's chest. She looks like a child. Sad, small, afraid.

"Come on. Let's go." Dad leads me past the kitchen and up the stairs. He looks back toward Mom, and his face reflects my confusion and worry. "Try to get some rest," he says, but he's distracted.

"Dad? What's going on?"

"Not sure … I'm sure everything's all right."

"What was Mom talking about? Who's Steven? And why was she talking about me?" The questions explode from me faster than I can even formulate them.

It's obvious that Dad doesn't know what to say.

"Let's chat in the morning." He kisses my forehead, takes my crutches, leans them up against the wall. His motions are slow and deliberate, like he's trying to stay calm.

"But—"

He rubs my arm, a little too hard.

"Enough for tonight," he says, probably more firmly than he intended to. "Good night, kiddo. I love you."

He closes the door on his way out.

I get into bed and pull the covers up over my head. She said Steven and Meranda and Mark. Does all of this have something to do with me? Is that why everyone is tiptoeing around me and avoiding my questions? How am I involved in this?

Crewmate Angus MacDonald recalls the harrowing event in haunting detail. "Then suddenly, these great hairy arms grabbed him from behind and pulled him toward the water. Steven tried to fight, but the arms were too strong. I ran to him and tried to pry him free, but those hands were like claws. Scratched my face and chest, here. We were no match for the selkie, and he dragged Steven off the deck and 'neath the waves. Never surfaced again."

***Legends of the Lakes* by Sarah Chapman, 2010**

Chapter 14

I wake to the sound of clinking glass and muffled radio voices. As I make my way downstairs, Dad hears my footsteps and looks up.

"G'morning, sunshine." He's got a garbage bag of bottles in one hand and is dragging a chair back to where it belongs with the other. "Sleep well?"

"I did," I answer, surprised. "You?"

"A bit short but not bad otherwise."

The image of Mom and Grampa from last night flashes in my mind. "Is Mom all right?"

"She's pretty tired, but she'll be fine. Try not to worry, 'kay?"

"'Kay," I lie.

"Grampa's in the kitchen. I bet he'll make you some breakfast," Dad says and continues with his bottle collecting, humming along with the theme song of a CBC Radio show.

"Oatmeal?" Grampa asks before I even have a chance to say good morning. He's probably been up for hours.

"Sounds great," I say.

He spoons me out some piping hot oats and sprinkles brown sugar and cinnamon on top. Putting the bowl on the counter in front of me, he says, "It'll stick to your ribs and warm you from the inside." Then he heads out to the living room, where I hear him sink into his armchair and open the newspaper.

I wrap my hands around the warm bowl, put my nose in the swirl of steam rising out. My senses grasp onto the comfort coming from the simple breakfast. That's Grampa. Simple comfort and warmth, with a touch of sugar.

The creaking of the wooden floors above me announces that Mom's up. More creaking as she comes down the stairs. I notice my white knuckles gripping the warm bowl and realize that I'm afraid to see her this morning. I don't know who to expect to walk into the kitchen: my mom, paranoid but decisive, or the other woman, jumpy and afraid. The one who's keeping things from me.

"Morning, sweetie." I can't tell yet. She's moving slowly. Her body looks weary and her blue eyes float in dark circles. She pours a cup of coffee and sits down next to me at the counter, staring at the steam rising from her mug.

"I saw police lights last night," I say.

"Yes, you did." Mom lowers her head and starts to pick at her cuticles. "Molly—I mean Detective Sullivan—came to give us some updates on the investigation. No news, really, but tough to listen to someone talk about Mark like that. Going over his final moments again and again."

The phone rings, and Mom stands quickly to answer it.

"Hello? Oh, hi, Sarah. Uh, I … no … I'd really prefer if … really? Let me think about it a minute and let you know. I know. All right." She hangs up, her face serious.

"What's wrong, Beth?" Dad must have heard the phone. "You okay?"

Mom sighs. "Sarah just called and wondered if Meranda could meet Claire in town, to go for ice cream. They'll be there for something else this afternoon, and Sarah wants you to drop Meranda at the shop later."

"And …?" Dad's confused.

"*And* I don't want the girls wandering on their own around town." Mom looks sternly at Dad.

"We'll be fine," I offer. "Not like we can possibly get lost in this tiny place, even if we tried." Dad grins at me, but there isn't a hint of a smile from Mom.

"It's just not safe," she says to Dad, like I'm completely invisible—or irrelevant to the discussion. "I'd feel much better knowing they were at Sarah and Jim's. Inside."

"Beth, I get it, I do. But we have to be reasonable here. The girls will stay together—right, Meranda? And—"

"You'd have to promise to stay away from the water. Can I trust you with that, Meranda? I mean it. Away from the water, away from the pier. Got it?" Mom looks like she may cry again.

"Got it, Mom. I got it." Who is this fearful woman?

She takes a deep breath, looks at Dad, and nods. Resigned.

It's Grampa who drives me into town after lunch. He has been tasked with picking up food for the reception after the funeral tomorrow. I'm happy to have him to myself for a little while—and happy to not have to help with more house cleanup.

The clouds sit low and hover above the lake like the fluffy duvet on my bed at home. The air is still and silent apart from the occasional birdcall from somewhere in the hidden treetops. We're barely out of the driveway when I turn to Grampa and blurt, "So, mermaids, huh?"

He turns his head quickly in my direction and studies my face. "Mermaids," he echoes, giving away nothing.

"Is it really true?" I ask him more pointedly.

He looks worried, like he's not sure what he's allowed to say. "You've heard the stories," he says. "We've been telling you since you were a baby."

"Uh, not really," I say with a bit of a laugh. "You've told me mermaid yarns and the legend of Malcolm McKenzie. I'd say you've downplayed the violent, evil mermaid angle a bit."

He stops at the town's only traffic light and rolls down the window. The air is saltier here than it was at the bakery yesterday. Laced with the smells of diesel and tar, it's strangely comforting. He looks at me, winks, and says, "Not exactly bedtime story material for a little one, now, is it?" He chuckles.

We wait at the light, the truck humming quietly under us. Grampa inhales the damp air through his nose. He's staring into the distance, toward the water.

I persevere. "What did the police say to Mom last night?"

"Well now, can't get anything by you, eh?" He rubs the whiskers on his cheeks wearily. "It seems the witness has changed some of his story. Probably doesn't change much in the end, but Molly just wanted the news to come from her. This town is known for being, well, chatty. Here we are."

He pulls into a parking spot. Claire is sitting on the curb in front of Baby Guppies Ice Cream and Candy Shoppe, her backpack between her legs. She waves when she sees us and meets me at the passenger door.

"Here, let me help," she says.

"Thanks." I hand her my crutches and lean on the door

handle to get out of the truck. I can tell that she's trying not to stare at my legs as I move. I take the crutches from her and make my way over the curb.

She sticks her head through the passenger window to talk to Grampa. "Grandma said she'd pick us up around four. Is that okay?"

"Sure, Claire, that'd be great." Then he yells over, "Bye, Meranda-girl. You gals enjoy your afternoon."

Claire turns to me, already opening the door to the shop. "Ice cream?" she asks.

Walking into Baby Guppies Ice Cream and Candy Shoppe is like walking into a scene from a cartoon. The walls are bright orange, with a pattern of tiny fish scales meticulously painted in black on all four walls. Behind the ice cream counter are two giant fish eyes and gills painted in the same black. There are rows of clear plastic bins filled with bulk candy, and I can't help but notice most of them are in the shape of sea creatures. Sour fish, gummy octopuses, fish-eye gumballs, chocolate starfish. The giant orange fish on the wall smiles at us as a teenage boy emerges from the back of the shop. Dressed in orange, he's almost camouflaged—with the exception of the plush orange fish hat. The mouth is the hole for his head, so it looks like a tropical fish is chewing on him. I try not to stare. Or laugh.

“Hey, Sean,” Claire says.

“Heya, Claire-Bear,” he says. “What can I getcha?”

“You remember my brother from the wake?” Claire asks, rolling her eyes. “Sean, this is Meranda. Visiting from out West. Meranda, this is Sean, aka Fish Bait.” She makes a face and points to Sean’s hat.

“Hey, Meranda,” says Sean, ignoring her quip. He’s not acting like the grumpy boy that snubbed us all at the door.

“Mint chocolate chip for me, please.” Claire mercifully interrupts the awkward silence.

“Same for me.”

Sean hands us our cones and tips his fish hat. Then he’s serious. “Best not eat those on the pier,” he says. “Grandma will kill you—if the merfolk don’t getcha first!” He laughs, clearly pleased with his joke.

“See what I mean?” Claire says as we leave the shop. “The town goes nutso.”

Chapter 15

"See any mermaids out there?" I ask with a giggle. We're sitting on a bench across the street from the pier, watching the water and eating ice cream. No response from Claire. Her face is frozen, staring ahead. She's far away. "Uh, hello?" Nothing. I try again. "Look! Mermaid!"

That does it. She blinks. "Huh?"

"You all right? You were a million miles away."

"Uh, sorry. I, uh … sorry." She's suddenly very interested in the drips on the side of her cone.

"What's up?"

"Nothing. Just family stuff, no biggie." She looks away.

"'Kay." If she doesn't want to talk, I won't push.

But then she starts. "My folks. I told you they're away for their anniversary, right? That's true, but the real reason they're away is my mom. She's been … unwell."

"Unwell?"

"She's got depression. Dad says it's a sickness, like having diabetes or cancer. Except it makes her sad. Makes her disappear. It's making our *family* disappear." Her voice is quiet, halting.

"Is she going to be all right?" I've heard about depression but have never met anyone with it.

Claire won't meet my eyes. She's staring at her feet. "She takes medicine for it, but Dad says it takes a long time to kick in. They're seeing a specialist in Halifax this week. Grandma says this doctor is one of the best. Even Mom seems hopeful. We'll see."

I'm not sure what to say. I've been feeling invisible to my family this week, but I can't imagine how it would feel to have Mom fade away or disappear. "At least you've got Sean, though, right? You're in this together."

Claire almost spits out her ice cream. "Yeah, right!" She wipes her lips with her sleeve. "Only thing Fish Bait is good for is keeping Mom and Dad outta my business. He gets into enough trouble that they pretty much leave me to my own devices. Apparently, I'm trustworthy." She makes a solemn face and puts her hand on her heart, then laughs.

"Must be nice," I say, imagining what my life would be like if my parents were too busy worrying about someone else to hover over me. Claire's face falls, and I realize I've just put my foot in my mouth. “I mean, to have a brother. Not your mom having depression.” Crap.

“Whatever.” She’s done talking about this. I ruined the moment. “Oh, I almost forgot.” She steers the conversation onward before I can say anything else. “I brought you a present.” Claire licks her sticky fingers, opens her backpack, and hands me a newspaper clipping.

I unfold the clipping and find the article I saw on the kitchen counter the day before. Uncle Mark’s grin leaps from the page under the headline. This time, I’m actually able to read the story.

Mark McKenzie, 68, of Skye, was pulled lifeless from the waters off Kettle Bay on Sunday afternoon. Crewmates report he was last seen at the stern of the vessel, untangling line. Minutes later, he was noted to be missing and was found floating several metres away. “I heard a sound like a kind of a holler, then a scraping noise,” recalls Angus MacDonald. “Then he was nowhere to be seen. I sounded the alarm and that’s when we saw his slicker floating in the waves.” McKenzie’s body was pulled from the water, and the crew performed CPR until met by rescue personnel on shore. He was pronounced dead on the pier. Authorities are investigating the incident.

"See?" says Claire. "Fishing accident."

"That's not what it says," I answer. "No one saw what actually happened. Plus, the police were at our house last night. Dad says one of the witnesses has changed his story."

"Who, Gus?" Claire asks with a smirk. "No surprise there. No one believes a thing that old kook says anyways."

I wait for her to explain.

She wrinkles her nose. "He claims to be the only one who has 'seen' a mermaid in ten years." Again, more air quotes. "What did he say, anyway?"

"I dunno, Mom wouldn't talk about it. Big surprise."

"Maybe it's in today's paper," Claire says, getting up from the bench. "We could go to the library and check it out?"

"Yes. Let's." If my family won't tell me what's going on, then I'll have to figure it out myself.

"Right then, let's go." She stands, grabs my crutches, and waits. "It's just a block down, on the other side of the street."

I hook my crutches onto my arms and follow Claire to the crosswalk. There are no vehicles on this stretch of road and the sole traffic light in town, two blocks away, is red. We arrive on the other side to find ourselves facing the pier. The air smells even stronger this close to the water: diesel, salt, and rubber. Grampa's smell. There are two boats docked that bob slightly below the height of the pier. One, a large lobster boat with a hydraulic hauler named *Stormy Skye*. I know this is the one that Uncle Mark worked on. The other is much smaller. It has three benches facing forward, bolted to the open deck, like a makeshift theater. On the front, I can make out the outline of a mermaid pointing forward, hair billowing behind. The words "Gus's Mermaid Watching Tours" are painted in gold along the side.

"Speak of the devil," Claire muttered.

"Wait, this is *Gus*? The one from the wake? I thought he was a fisherman, not … a mermaid tour guide."

"Runs this tourist trap in his spare time when he's not out on the fishing boat. Tourist season's winding down now so looks like he's starting to close up shop." Claire points to a pile of wooden signs next to the boat. "Wanna take a detour and check it out?"

Yes, I do. I really, really do. But I imagine the conversation with Mom and Dad if they find out I went onto the pier, especially after the drama at the house before I left. I imagine what would happen if I slipped or tripped and fell off the edge. No adult here to grab me. I don't want to tell Claire that I'm not supposed to. Or that I'm afraid to. I'm such a baby sometimes. "My legs are a bit tired today, best not to take any detours," I lie. "Library?"

"Okay, then." Claire pauses, her eyes drifting upwards. "Uh-oh." She points at the dark clouds moving in from the lake. "Where'd those come from? We'd better boot it 'fore the skies open up and we get soaked!"

"Get away! Get away from here!" A voice booms over a gust of wind. We whirl around to find its source. A man in a bright yellow rain slicker is leaning over the pier, thrusting a pole or an oar into the water. Splashes erupt from below the edge. The man turns and sees Claire and me watching him from the street.

"You girls! Don't get any closer. Stay away! Far away!" It's Gus. He thrashes the oar into the water again. "Selkie. Bold enough to come right up to the edge. He'd better not come back, I tell you."

My guts sink and splash like the whitecaps in the distance. A selkie? A mermaid? Here? Gus looks so afraid. I'm momentarily conflicted—wanting to run to the water's edge to help and maybe even see the mystical creature I don't officially believe in versus wanting to run for safety.

"Should we help him?" I ask. "He looks frightened. What if—?"

Claire snorts. "Whatever. Weirdo." She tosses her hair, turns her back to Gus and the pier, and continues along the sidewalk. Then she looks back at me. "Don't even give him the time of day," she says. "Always tryin' to drum up business, that one. Dad calls him a shark. Says he preys on the fantasies of tourists. Let's go."

I don't know. Gus holds the oar over his shoulder, bracing for another jab, his eyes wide in terror. I begin to make my way toward him, then he looks directly at me. "Especially you, Mer-girl," he growls. "Best be staying clear of the water."

A crash of thunder rocks my body as if the sound came from inside me. I drop one of my crutches. By the time I've bent down to grab it and stood up again, the rain has started. Claire takes off, running for cover under the awning of the hardware store at the beginning of the block. She doesn't look back. Clearly, in a reflexive moment, she forgot about my legs. I'm used to being left behind, but my body still tenses up in anger, and my legs get clumsy. It takes me longer than it should to catch up, and I can feel Claire's eyes on me when I stumble over the curb and onto the sidewalk. Raindrops pelt my face and thankfully hide the tears of frustration that have escaped. I want to throw my crutches in the gutter and scream. I want to scream so loud and long that it echoes off the lake and hills in an endless roar that would be impossible to ignore. A roar so loud that no one can push it aside or deny it. I want to grab the world by the shoulders and shake it, howling, *I'm here! I'm not fragile, I can handle this. Let me in!* I picture Mom's face in that moment. She'd be shocked by this hurricane force inside me. I wish she could see it, but the more I think of her, the more my noiseless scream shrinks.

Someday. Someday she'll have to see it, and I'll burst out of this bubble they keep me in. But not today. Not here, where Mom is so sad and scared. When I join Claire under the dark green awning, I'm more out of breath than I should be from rushing in out of the rain. I've swallowed my roar, to save for another time.

"Sorry," Claire says. "I guess I shoulda waited for you."

"I'm fine," I snap at her. "I don't need help or anything." It comes out meaner than I intend. "No worries, seriously. I'm good." I force the words out through clenched teeth.

Up until recently, the town of Skye enjoyed a spectacularly low rate of injuries and fatalities as compared to fishing towns of a similar size. Between 1900 and 2008, there were no water-related deaths reported involving Skye residents and very few injuries. There were no significant differences in background weather patterns, boating technology, or town population throughout that period of over a century that could explain this phenomenon. In the last two years, however, beginning with the violent death of Steven Kirkland, the town has experienced a spike in the reported injuries and incidents on the water.

***Legends of the Lakes* by Sarah Chapman, 2010**

Chapter 16

The rain is really pelting down now, but the block before the library is lined with shops that all have colorful awnings over the sidewalk, so we walk at a comfortable pace. The air is sweet with the smell of rain and wet leaves, and it starts to soothe my anger, settling it back down deep where it belongs. Claire turns off the sidewalk, and I follow her up the steps to the library. It's a single-story red brick building that looks newer than most of the rest of the town. We walk in, and the beautiful scent of old books fills my lungs and melts away what is left of my dark mood. I close my eyes for a second to let the smell crash over me until I'm submerged. I could float away.

"Prepare yourself," Claire whispers. "The librarian is Gus's wife. She's not creepy like him, but she chatters more than the gulls when the fishin' boats come in." She walks straight to the desk. "Hi, Mrs. MacDonald, have you got today's *Gazette*?"

"Oh, hello, Claire, dear." Mrs. MacDonald is a short, round lady with wildly frizzy hair and laughing eyes. When she talks, her voice is a giggle. "There should be a couple of copies on the reading table over there. Whatcha lookin' for?"

Claire ignores the question. "'Kay, thanks!" She waves me over to a table across from the librarian's desk. I count four stacks of shelves on each side of the long narrow room. It looks like there would be barely enough space between them to browse the books. In the far corner sits a small table with an old desktop computer and in the other corner are two faded armchairs. The whole library is hardly the size of the kids' section of my local library at home. Claire and I find sections of newspapers from the last two days scattered on the tabletop and start weeding through stories about community potlucks, garage sale notices, and an article featuring Beatrice from Kettle O' Fish Bakery and Café selling her famous pumpkin pies to be ordered for Thanksgiving.

"Found it!" I lay out the spread with Uncle Mark's face beside the byline.

Investigation into Fisherman's Death Continues

Local detectives continue to probe into the death of Mark McKenzie, whose body was pulled from the lake last week.

Crew members previously stated that no one had seen McKenzie fall overboard, but new evidence has surfaced. "We have two witnesses that claim they heard voices on deck just before the victim disappeared," says Detective Sullivan. "And one witness heard a scream." McKenzie's death has rekindled superstition in some locals who fear the legend of the Bras d'Or mermaids. Believers blame the mermaids for the nearly decade-long increase in injuries and deaths in and around the waters off Skye. This fear has led to acts of vandalism this week targeting images of the legendary sea creatures, including some of Skye's most famous tourist attractions. Autopsy results are expected later this week. Sullivan asks that anyone with information about McKenzie's death or about property destruction please contact local police.

"I saw one of these," I say, when we finish reading. "The statue at the post office. It was nearly destroyed."

"And someone spray-painted the side of the school," says Claire. "We noticed it on the way home from your grandparents' place last night."

"Find what you need, girls?" It's the cheery voice of Mrs. MacDonald. She peers over Claire's shoulder to see what we're reading and clucks her tongue. "Such a shame. That poor, poor family. I hear that even Beth—" She stops talking, looks at my crutches and then at me. "Ah, of course," she says, nodding slowly, "you must be Gwenn Campbell's granddaughter." I feel my cheeks flush a little. The crutches are like a birthmark, only it's a mark I can never conceal. "The miracle baby returned home at last! How is your mother? I can't even remember the last time I saw her. Must have been before the tragedy, before she left for the mainland."

Did she just say "tragedy"? What tragedy? I want to ask her what she means, but she keeps talking.

"She was quite the regular in here back in the day. What a reader she was. Is she well?" She pauses. I open my mouth to answer what I thought was a question, but she keeps going, as if I'm not even here. "I hear the wake was lovely. My Gus tells me it was well attended, which is so nice. I was so sorry to have missed it. My mother, you see, she's not well and I needed to be with her in Baddeck. Will you give my regards to your grandmother? I'll see her tomorrow at the funeral, of course. Please tell her that I'm here, and if there's anything she needs ..." I wait. It's not a question, but she looks at me expectantly.

"I will tell her," I say. "Thank you."

The phone rings, and Mrs. MacDonald startles. "Oooh,

excuse me, ladies." She giggles and goes back to the desk.

Claire smiles and rolls her eyes, and I hold my breath to stifle a laugh.

"Probably better go soon. Grandma's got a thing about punctuality. Says being late is the ultimate form of rudeness," Claire says, in a high-pitched voice, sitting up extra-straight. She gets up and takes her backpack off the back of the chair. I slide my chair out and get my arms into my crutches before lifting myself up.

"Gus says the storm is still growin' out there." Mrs. MacDonald is off the phone and peering out the window at the front of the building. "It's as dark as night," she says. "You girls aren't walking home, are ya?" She stares at my crutches again, her head cocked to one side.

"Nah, my grandma's coming to get us," Claire says, her hand on the door. "Thanks!" And she's gone.

"Nice to meet you," I say, trying to be polite as I follow her outside.

"Bye!" Mrs. MacDonald calls as the door closes.

"Sorry," Claire says, "that woman talks so much it makes me want to run. Needs to fill any quiet space with words. So many words. Weird for a librarian, huh?"

We laugh about that as we descend the steps and start

walking down the block back to the ice cream shop to meet Claire's grandma. The rain has stopped, but the wind is howling and ringing the bells on the buoys in the water.

"Can you imagine what it's like at home? No wonder Gus is so weird. He probably never gets a chance to speak, then just doesn't know what to do when his wife's not around! Come to think of it, that explains a lot." Claire grins. "Could be why he spends so much of his time on boats. Fishing and 'mermaid tours.'" She says the last two words sarcastically.

We're walking by the pier when the streetlights come on. "Yikes, it feels like ten o'clock at night," I say, trying not to let on that I'm a bit creeped out by this weather.

"Crazy," Claire agrees. "Almost there."

The boats creak and whine, pushed and pulled by the waves, thumping against the bumpers on the pier, sending pillars of water into the air and onto the dock like cannon fire. I raise my voice to be heard over the din. "Did you hear what the library lady said? She said Mom and Dad left 'after the tragedy.' What was she talking about? And before, did you hear Gus call me Mer-girl?"

A horn pierces the air, and we both jump. A bright blue VW Beetle pulls up to the curb beside us.

"Hop in, girls, 'fore the floods start!" It's Claire's grandma.

Heavy drops bounce off the roof of the car and splash onto my face. Slowly at first, but within seconds, a sheet of rain sends me clambering inside. Claire and I look at each other as the rain pelts down and smile: just in time.

"Whatcha girls get up to?" Claire's grandma's green eyes peer at us from behind red-framed glasses in the rearview mirror. I had thought her hair was gray when I met her at Gran and Grampa's, but I see now looking at the back of her head that it is laced with red, like it was once the same shade as Claire's. She's wrapped from chin to chest in a thick black knit scarf, worn over her black raincoat. "Did you get wet?"

"Not really," Claire answers. "We already finished our ice cream when the weather turned. Then we hid safe and snug in the library."

"Get any books?"

"Nah, mostly chatted and browsed." Claire puts her finger to her lips. She doesn't want to tell her grandmother what we were doing. It would seem to me that her grandma might be exactly the person who could help us. She knows more about the mermaid stuff than anyone. Claire must see that I'm contemplating, so she narrows her eyes and again puts her finger to her lips. "Not worth it," she mumbles through clenched teeth.

"What's that now?" The green eyes in the mirror.

“Nothing, Grandma.” Claire elbows me.

Claire’s grandma pulls the car into a parking spot by the pier to turn around. As we drive away, I notice that Gus is gone. His boat is bobbing and tossing in the waves. The mermaid on the front looks like she’s dancing. Her outstretched arm is reaching for me. Beckoning.

Chapter 17

The front door of the house opens, and Mom jogs toward the car, opening an umbrella. She ducks down to wave at Claire's grandma through the car window, then helps me open my door, holding the umbrella over me as I get out and adjust my crutches. I notice that she looks more like herself. Tired but a bit more relaxed. The rain starts to pound down in heavy drops that splash up dirt from the driveway on our way to the porch.

"Ooooh! Those are cold drops!" Mom giggles. She puts her arm around my waist and squeezes, her eyes smiling. For that second, we're us again. Without secrets or tension.

But then, "Oh, sweetie, I'm so glad you're home safe. I—"

I snap before I can stop myself. "Safe? From what, angry mermaids? Of course I am." And I walk inside in front of her.

My legs are throbbing, aching. Half an hour later, after sitting down to dinner, the pain is distracting. I find myself imagining the relief of plunging my legs into the cool water of the lake. I look around the table at my family, these people who have been the center of my universe, my source of strength and truth, and it's like seeing them from underwater. They're above the surface, and I'm under, looking up at them on the other side. They're distorted, out of reach, secrets floating between us. We're all feeling it, I think.

"Quite the storm surge this afternoon, eh?" Dad wades in. You can always count on him to fill an uncomfortable silence. "Anyone see that comin'?"

"Wasn't in any forecast we saw this morning, isn't that right, Gwenn?" Gran and Grampa seem grateful for the small talk. "I hear the Sullivans had a tree come down and just miss their house."

"And we'll have some work to do clearing branches and leaves from the lawn." Grampa and Dad continue to discuss the yard work before I decide to speak.

"Someone called me 'Mer-girl' today," I blurt.

They look surprised, but no one says anything. "Anyone know what that means? Or care to tell me?"

Gran shoots Mom a look, then smiles patiently, apparently deciding to ignore my rudeness.

"Oh, honey," she says warmly. "Grampa and I talk about you

so much that I bet the whole town feels like they know you. Maybe whoever this was couldn't quite remember your name. Y'know, Mer-anda, Mer-girl, not that much of a stretch."

But Mom looks suspicious. "Who was it?" she asks.

Here we go.

"Gus," I tell her.

"Gus MacDonald?" She looks at me accusingly. "Where did you see Gus?"

"He yelled it at me from the pier as we were walking to the library. Don't worry, Mom, we weren't near the water." My voice is getting louder, annoyance bubbling in my gut, rising like lava. "Can I please be excused?" I'm crawling out of my skin and want to be alone for a while.

They look surprised again. Guess I'm full of surprises today.

"You sure?" Gran asks. "You didn't eat much."

I feel bad for snapping but not bad enough to talk about it.

"It's okay. I'm just tired. My legs hurt. I think I'll head up to bed."

"Your legs have been bothering you a lot the last few days." Mom looks worried. "I can tell by how you move. Do you want—?"

I cut her off. "It's fine. Probably from running from the storm today." But she's right; they've been aching more and more since we arrived.

Silence. They don't know what to do with me. Truth be told,

neither do I. I push out from the table, pull myself up on my crutches, and cross the dining room. "Good night, everyone," I say on my way by.

Mom meets me at the bottom of the stairs, blocking my way up. "Sleep well, sweetheart. I'll come check on you in a bit." She leans closer and her sweatshirt smells so much like home that tears prickle my eyes. I realize I miss her. I never dreamed that once we came to Cape Breton I'd ever want to go home. But I do. Home to our life before. Before the secrets.

I decide to try one last time—to clear the air between us. "Mom? The librarian called me a miracle baby too."

She sighs, and it looks like she is gritting her teeth in frustration. Then she forces a smile, smooths my hair from my face, and says, "You know what that means, sweetheart. We talked about this—your dad and I had been trying for so long when you came along. You are our miracle." She covers my birthmark with her hand, to stop me from rubbing it.

I know that is the truth, but it isn't the *whole* truth. Hard to believe the local librarian cared about Mom and Dad's dreams of a baby. And she had mentioned a "tragedy." The distance between Mom and me just keeps getting bigger.

Mom kisses my forehead. "We'll get through this, I promise. I love you." For a split second, I want to throw myself into her arms, bury myself in her. But I don't. The moment passes. She moves out of my way, and I go upstairs into my room and close the door behind me.

Exhausted, I flop down on the bed, crutches and all, breathing in the faintly dusty smell of the quilt, my glasses partially off my face. I need to figure out what happened to Uncle Mark. If I can do that, then Mom will come back to us. Things can go back to normal. When I roll over, I notice the cover of *Legends of the Lakes* next to my face. Rolling onto my back and straightening my glasses, I flip through my beloved book. The map of the Bras d'Or Lake, Malcolm McKenzie's clock, photos of fishing boats on the pier, the photo of a middle-aged man in a slicker and winter cap.

I sit up and look closer. I know this photo well, but now I *recognize* this man. It's Gus. He's younger, but it's definitely him. My eyes drop to the caption beneath the photo: *Angus MacDonald claims to have witnessed the first mermaid attack in 2008.* Gus is Angus MacDonald. I can't believe I didn't put this together before now. Angus MacDonald, who saw a mermaid grab his crewmate Steven Kirkland and pull him to his death. *The only mermaid sighting in almost ten years*—that's what Claire had said earlier. Now he's had another crewmate die in front of him. No wonder he's losing it. His rant at the wake makes a bit more sense to me now, and I feel sorry for him.

I close the book and put it in the drawer in the bedside table, feeling somewhat satisfied that I've managed to piece something together on my own. I can't wait to tell Claire tomorrow. When I lay the book in the drawer, my fingers graze something on the bottom. I pull it out. It's a gold necklace. On the end of the chain a round pendant glimmers in the evening light. A circle with a tiny tail curled inside.

Chapter 18

Man, I hate tights. I don't think I have ever in my life had a pair that have actually fit me. Actually, I don't think properly fitting tights are a real thing. They either sag at the crotch and fall down relentlessly or they bunch at the knees like elephant legs. And how has no one figured out how to make an itch-free version? Maybe that will be how I get rich one day. Itch-free tights that fit.

I'm struggling to do up the button at the back of my dress when Gran walks by my room.

"Oh, Meranda, don't you look nice." She stands in the door frame for a moment. "I had a flicker of a memory of your mother. It feels like a lifetime since this room last loved a little girl." She steps into the room and runs her hand along the spines of the books on the shelf. "I think this house has needed you. And so have I." She swallows her tears, takes a deep breath, and helps me do up my button.

"You remind me of her so much," she says.

"Yeah, right," I say with a snort, putting my glasses on and flinging my dark hair over my shoulders. "Hardly."

Gran looks surprised by my reaction. "I wasn't talking about how you look," she says. "You're like her in more ways than you know. You're both kind, strong, curious, and not willing to take no for an answer. Even when maybe that would be the easiest way."

"Sure, then," I say, not wanting to talk about it anymore. "Ready?"

"As I'll ever be."

Everyone else is waiting by the door when we get downstairs. We all get into Grampa's truck and drive the uphill road to the church.

"So, Meranda," Mom starts. I'm still mad at her, but I swallow it down. Today is not the day. *Here goes*, I think—no big life event would be complete without a pep talk from Mom. Usually, it contains instructions that may have been helpful when I was five, like "Don't forget to say 'please' and 'thank you'" or "Remember your table manners." I know she's having a rough time, so I look at her and promise myself I won't roll my eyes. "When we get there, we'll be walked up the aisle to the front section of the church. We'll all sit together in the front pew. The pastor will speak, there will be songs, and Gran will give her eulogy. Just follow along, stand when everyone else stands, and you can sing along with the songs in the songbook."

I've never been to church. Mom and Dad were both brought up Presbyterian, but both stopped going to church when they left home. Dad, ever the scientist, says he stopped believing in God when his life's work became focused on evidence and fact. He told me once that he misses it sometimes: faith, magic. Mom says she's not sure what she believes, so we've never landed on any particular religious practice as a family. I nod somberly as Mom continues. "And it sounds like there'll be lots of people. Some you will have met at the wake the other night, but you'll be introduced to lots more. Remember to please look at people when they talk to you and try to use their names if you can."

I've heard this spiel before, but today it sounds like Mom is giving herself the pep talk, not me.

Grampa pulls into the parking lot, and we get out.

"Okay?" Mom says.

"Got it, Mom," I say. "You don't need to worry about me."

As we walk up the steps of the church, I steal a glance toward the cemetery. I can make out the fins on a few of the headstones in the distance framed by the glimmer of the lake behind them.

Sitting in the front pew between Mom and Dad, I feel as if we're the only ones in here. If it weren't for the occasional cough or sniffle from the abyss behind me, I'd swear we were alone with the casket. I can't help but stare. I imagine Uncle Mark lying in the dark wooden box. Is he in his work clothes? Or did someone dress him in a suit or something for this? The framed photo on top of the casket is the same one on the leaflet I saw at the Chowder House. The program that now sits in my lap. Uncle Mark's eyes and the pendant trigger a memory, and suddenly I'm swept into a cozy moment: I'm little, and I'm sitting on Gran's lap in our living room in Calgary. Snuggled up with a book. She leans over me as she's reading, and I reach up to touch the pendant dangling from her neck. "*Dìon maighdeann-mhara*," she says to me. She covers my little hands with hers around the pendant. "Always under the mermaid's protection." That's where I've seen the necklace before. Gran. But she hasn't worn it in years.

The pastor speaks directly to Gran, Uncle Mark's closest relative. We sit and listen, stand and listen, stand and sing, and kneel in quiet. Then Reverend Tim calls Gran to the altar to "say goodbye to her brother Mark."

Gran carefully climbs the carpeted steps to the altar and turns to face the crowd gathered behind us. This woman who is always so poised, so calm, looks rattled—like she's not quite sure how she ended up there. Then she meets Grampa's eye, takes a deep breath, and begins to speak.

"I'd like to start by reading part of a poem by Robert Louis Stevenson, a great Scotsman, whose words were read to us when we were kids and truly capture how I feel today.

> Give me again all that was there,
> Give me the sun that shone!
> Give me the eyes, give me the soul,
> Give me the lad that's gone!
> Sing me a song of a lad that is gone,
> Say, could that lad be I?
> Merry of soul he sailed on a day
> Over the sea to Skye.
> Billow and breeze, islands and seas,
> Mountains of rain and sun,
> All that was good, all that was fair,
> All that was me is gone."

The last word is merely a whisper. She clears her throat to continue, but I don't really hear anything else. I watch her face for the rest of the eulogy. Wrinkles frame her eyes in the same way Mom's do, but they're deeper. Deeper even than they were in the summer. For a fleeting second, I realize that she has gotten older. I'd assumed that time in Cape Breton stood still. That my grandparents floated in a bubble far away, their lives on pause until I'd see them again. That their lives were dependent on mine. The next emotion that floats to the surface is anger. I suddenly resent that I have been kept away from this place, from these people for so long. I can't believe my mom has done that to me. My curiosity to learn the truth about the mermaid legend turns to a deep need to understand this story, the story of my family. To not let anything come between me and this place again.

There is laughter from the invisible crowd behind me. Gran has finished a funny story about Uncle Mark. Her eyes are alight with love as her hand grazes the casket on her way back to our row. She smiles at all of us and joins our row like she's coming ashore. And I know how she feels.

Chapter 19

Waves of people spill out of the tiny church into the sunshine and cover the lawn, ebbing and flowing from the cemetery to the parking lot. Many of them hug Gran and Mom on the way out. Some pat my head or shoulder. Beatrice from the bakery stands next to Gran for a little too long, blowing her nose and wiping tears. Gran suddenly escapes the receiving line and makes her way through the crowds on the steps. She stops behind Kate, one of Mark's crewmates, and puts her hand on her shoulder. Kate turns, startled. Her face is blotchy, and there's mascara across her temple. Gran moves her hand to Kate's cheek, then gives her the framed photo of Uncle Mark from the church. Kate starts to cry and hugs Gran. She seems more upset than the rest of the crew. I wonder why.

"How's everyone holding up?" It's Kelly from the Chowder House. Mom turns from talking with an elderly man, and her eyes widen in surprise.

"Kelly? I wasn't expecting to see you here." Her cheeks flush pink. She makes her way down the steps, her eyes on her feet. "How nice of you to come."

Kelly shakes her head sadly. "After seeing you in the restaurant the other day, I remembered how close we were once. If you'd told me fifteen years ago that it would have been unexpected for me to show up at your uncle Mark's funeral, I'd have said you were crazy." Her eyes are moist, threatening to overflow. "And if you'd told me that you would leave town and cut all ties completely, I'd have said you were plain certifiable. But here we are. And here you are. After eight years."

Mom is picking at her fingers, three of which still have bandages on them. "Kel, I'm sorry. I—"

"No, Beth," Kelly says. "I didn't come here to fight with you or to get answers. Who knows, maybe there'll be another time for that. I came today to show you and your family my support, that's all. Some connections last forever." She leans in and hugs Mom. Mom stiffens for a moment, then wilts in her old friend's arms. An old friend I'd never heard mentioned before we got out here.

"Thanks, Kelly. I miss you too."

Out of the corner of my eye I see movement in the cemetery. I recognize the hunched silhouette of the groundskeeper, Alex, as he makes his way up the hill, the afternoon sun reflecting on the lake behind him. Between Mom and Kelly's emotional reunion and the funeral guests, no one will notice I'm gone for a few minutes, so I wander through the white headstones toward him.

"Mr. Duncan?" I call to him when I'm close enough. I don't want to frighten him and have him go over the edge.

"Hello?" he answers, looking around. Then he sees me. "Ahh, young Miss Campbell. How nice to see you again. Was it a good service?" He wanders to the bench and sits down.

"Yes, thanks," I say. "And it's Meranda. Morgan, actually, not Campbell." Never mind.

"Join me?" he asks, patting the seat beside him. There's no trace of the man who was so freaked out the last time I was here.

I sit, and we look over the water together for several minutes, the hum of voices from the church lawn behind us fading into the background. The wind is starting to pick up, and there are whitecaps on the surface of the lake that weren't there this morning. The leaves in the trees rustle, the long grass at the edge of the cliff ripples, and I can hear the flapping of the flag on the church steeple getting louder.

"I apologize for my behavior the other day," he says. "My demons sometimes rise to the surface when I least expect it.

Pain is a funny thing that way. Can hide so quietly, then blind us without warning."

I follow his gaze to a group of headstones slightly separated from the main cemetery, closer to the cliff's edge than the rest. The dates on the stones are all the same: August 19, 2010. I look back at Alex, waiting for an explanation.

"There lie the ones that didn't make it," he says. He gently takes my hand and raises my sleeve a bit to look at my birthmark. "Most days, I wish I hadn't. I live with the guilt every single day."

"What happened?" I ask him.

Alex drops my hand and turns to face me. His brown eyes reach deep into mine. "Come on, lass. You mean you don't know? How is that possible, you bein' who you are and all?"

I don't know what to say. Nothing.

"The ferry disaster. Worst day this town has ever seen. Twenty good souls lost, and some damaged forever beyond repair. I still dunno if this town will ever recover. Visions and sounds from that vessel as it pitched and creaked, they haunt me day and night."

"You were on the ferry?" I ask. "I'm so sorry. That must have been absolutely horrible."

"Aye, I was there." He raises his eyes to mine. "And so were you, m'dear."

"Ready, kiddo?" Dad asks from behind me. I wonder how long he's been there.

"Dad. I—" When I turn back to Alex, he's gone. His stooped frame moving across the grass back toward the church.

Dad is staring at the headstones from the ferry disaster. He looks from me to the figure of Alex getting smaller and back to me again.

"Uh, Dad?"

"Yes, kid?"

"Anything you'd like to tell me?"

It was one of those fogs that swallows ships whole. So thick that you'd swear you could feel it when you reached out your hand, that it would slow you down when you ran across the deck. Men aboard the crabbing vessel Outcast *could barely see the boots on their feet, let alone the shoreline. They knew that a lighthouse was out there somewhere, they could hear the foghorn, but saw no light to guide them. Captain Kevin Malone tried in vain to lower the anchor to wait for the fog to clear, but the winds picked up, lurching the* Outcast *toward certain wreckage. First Mate James McDermitt remembers, "Men were prayin' on the deck, bracin' for the crash onto the rocks. Then, splashes off the port bow. I looked down and saw what I thought was a dolphin or a whale—but then it waved an arm. Craziest thing. I hollered at the captain and we followed this creature's directions to shore. And safety. To this day, I'm not sure what I saw wasn't just a spirit but sure looked like a mermaid to me then."*

***Legends of the Lakes* by Sarah Chapman, 2010**

Chapter 20

In the car on the way back to Gran and Grampa's, I rest my head on Dad's shoulder. "Remember our deal," he whispers in my ear and kisses my head. Before Mom called us back from the cemetery, Dad had promised to tell me about the ferry. But only when the funeral day was over. "It's a big conversation, Meranda," he'd said, "and we have a job to do today for your mother and Gran. This story will keep."

I try to let my thoughts of the ferry and my anger about not having known sink down deep. I will have to float along the surface of the day to get through.

Mom and Gran discuss who was there and how nice the service was.

"The eulogy was so great, Gwenn," Dad says, leaning into the front seat. "You captured Mark perfectly. So many people said so."

"Thanks, Gabe. I owed him that, I think."

Claire and her grandparents, Sarah and Jim, are sitting on the porch when we get to the house. Claire's grandmother hands Gran a dish wrapped in foil. "Thanks, Sarah. Is this one of your pies?" Sarah doesn't answer. Instead, she smirks, mutters something under her breath, turns her back, and enters the house behind Grampa. Gran looks stung for a second, then holds her head high and follows them inside.

"Sean had to work this afternoon," Jim says, as if apologizing for his wife's behavior.

"You said some really nice things, Mrs. Campbell," Claire says to Gran.

"Thanks, dear." Gran and Claire chat about her parents for a few minutes, so I go into the living room to wait for her. Kate is sitting alone in one of the chairs facing the window. Her cheeks are wet.

"Oh, Meranda," she says, getting up when I come close. "I didn't hear you come in." She really must have been lost in thought if she didn't hear me and my crutches clumping along. She sits down on the couch and pats the seat beside her. I sit.

"Mark really did love you, you know," she says, smiling through damp eyes. "He talked about you like he saw you every day. Family meant so much to him. He used to imagine how things could have been if your family hadn't moved so far away."

I nod, not saying anything.

"We used to talk about coming out West for a visit … but now …" she trails off.

I can't help but notice her use of the word "we." Kate must have sensed that.

"Did you know we were about to announce our engagement? We were planning to tell everyone this week. Actually, we were in the midst of planning a bit of a party the night he left. He was so distracted that night, anxious. Said he had something to make right and then we'd get on to planning our lives. But …" Her words drift out the window, over the lake. Then she seems to remember I'm sitting beside her. "Oh my. Guess I got lost there for a moment. Sorry 'bout that. He was one in a million, your uncle." She wipes her nose with the edge of her sleeve and stands. "Best be seein' if your folks need help in the kitchen."

"Kate?" I say, my heart full of sadness for this stranger. "I'm glad he was so happy."

"Thanks, Meranda. I think we would have been," she says quietly. "I wish we could have been."

And she's gone, passing Claire on her way out of the living room.

Claire looks back at Kate. "What was *that* about?"

"She told me that she and Uncle Mark were engaged, but they

hadn't told anyone yet." I'm not sure why the idea of Uncle Mark getting married seems strange. Maybe because he was almost as old as Gran. I suppose old people can fall in love too. My heart sinks thinking of how Kate and Mark must have felt happy for a brief time, and now she is so lost without him.

Once a few more people arrive, and it looks like we won't be missed, Claire and I sneak up to my room.

She plunks down on the blue quilt and tosses her backpack onto the floor with a thump. "I hate funerals," she says with a sigh as she lies back on the bed. "Don't you?"

"My first," I say like I am admitting a dark secret.

She sits up and studies me like she's trying to tell if I'm kidding. Then she cocks her head to the side and says, "I'm a pro. My parents know a lot of old people. That's what comes of never leaving the place you grew up in. Your folks had the right idea."

I nod distractedly, but my mind is somewhere else. I have to ask her, so I blurt out, "Did you know about the ferry disaster? Did you know I was on it?" The questions won't stop. "Why has no one ever told me that? What caused it? How many survivors were there? Why has no one ever told me? Why? Why?" I'm crying. I can't breathe. My insides are exploding. It's all coming out now, like I can't keep it contained another moment.

Claire jumps off the bed and is at my side. Her hand is on my shoulder, and she is speaking in my ear, but she sounds so far away.

"Okay, okay," she's saying. "It's okay. It's going to be all right. Do you want me to call your mom? Or dad?"

"No. Not them." I shake my head. "Not now. I don't think I want to see them. I'm so confused, so angry, so …" I can't stop crying.

Claire stands in front of me with her hands on her hips. "All right then. We will figure this out without them. But first, I need you to calm down. Now sit."

I do.

"Breathe."

I do.

"Good." She puts her hands on my shoulders. "Ready?"

"Yes, I think so." I wipe my eyes, dry my face with my sleeve. Take another breath.

"What do you want to know?" Claire asks.

"Everything."

She sits next to me on the bed. "Okay, I'll tell you what I know. But I'm going to start by telling you that I seriously thought you knew about this already. I mean, OMG, how could you not? I wasn't keeping a secret, just assumed you didn't want to talk about it. It's not like we knew each other well or anything."

I nod. No words. Waiting for her to continue.

"It happened the summer I was three," Claire begins. "There used to be a ferry that would take you across the long part of the lake between Skye and Halkirk. It ran twice a day and one night, on the way back to Skye, a big storm rolled in. People said they felt a big bump or a crash and the whole ferry tilted to one side and started to take on water. Apparently, it sank in minutes. Most people didn't have time to get to the lifeboats or even get life jackets. So many people died. It was awful, they say. We have a ceremony every summer to remember. There's a monument out near where the ferry used to dock. It's an angel."

"And I was on the ferry?" It's hard to imagine—this sounds like a horrible scene from a movie, not my actual life.

"Yes. I guess you and your mom were coming home from visiting an aunt or friend or someone. You were actually missing for a while. They found you hours and hours later after a huge search. On the shoreline. Apparently, you were totally fine. A miracle, really."

"Miracle baby," I whisper.

"Huh?"

"That's what the librarian called me, remember? 'Miracle baby.' This is what she meant."

Thoughts and images are swirling in my head. I close my eyes tight and try to shake them out of my mind. How can this story be true? How have I not been told this before? As I let it sink in, some things begin to come into focus.

"Is that why Alex and Sandy knew who I was?"

"I guess your birthmark was part of the description they gave everyone to find you that night. You're kinda famous around here. Like a real-life legend. And the fact that you all left so quickly adds to the mystery too, I suppose. They say that mermaids were involved. The official cause was the sudden storm surge, but folks were so angry. It was not that long after Steven Kirkland was killed, then this. And if they weren't to blame for the sinking, folks couldn't understand why the mermaids didn't come to the people's rescue. Alex Duncan says he saw mermaids there that night."

"Alex, the cemetery guy?"

Claire nods. "Yes, he was the captain. He survived but has never set foot on a boat since. Messed him up pretty bad that he survived and so many didn't. And my grandmother lost her best friend. If she didn't hate the McKenzies before the accident, she sure did then."

I don't even have to ask.

"Grandma's always goin' on about how the McKenzies think they're so much better than the rest of us. The legend of mermaid protection and all." She rolls her eyes. "I think it was an issue even back to when your grandfather and grandmother started dating. Didn't like the idea of grandpa's best friend hangin' with the McKenzie crew. Mom says that it all got worse after Steven Kirkland was killed. That was the final straw for Grandma, I guess." Claire stops talking and turns to look at me. Again, realizing that I may have absolutely no idea what she's talking about, she adds, "You know, Steven Kirkland?"

"Steven …" I say, remembering what Mom had said the other night in the kitchen. And then it clicks. "Steven Kirkland from the book? The first to be killed by merfolk? He was a friend of our grandparents?"

"I know, right?" she continues. "Steven, my grandpa, and your grandfather were best friends. Families practically grew up together, I guess. He owned Kirkland's, the biggest fishing company in Skye. He died when I was little. Horrible, apparently. His body washed up and was barely recognizable. Maimed, they say."

"I know this story," I interject. "Gus was there that night too. He said a mermaid grabbed Steven right off the deck."

"Right," Claire answers. "Claimed he tried to fight him off but was no match. Got himself pretty beat up in the scuffle but wasn't able to save Steven. And then somehow you survived the ferry accident, like you found your own way to shore. When Mark died, Grandma said it was high time this curse hit the McKenzie clan as well as the rest of us."

I'm not sure what to say. This place is full of mysteries. And sadness. And anger. And everyone is connected by it somehow. Including me.

Then a knock on the door signals it's time for Claire to go.

"Better not make them wait," she says, packing up her stuff. "Sorry to dump so much on you and run out. How much longer you here?"

"We leave Sunday."

"'Kay. I'll call you tomorrow." She hugs me, then she dashes down the stairs.

Chapter 21

I'm soaring. Flying. No, gliding. It's dark, and I'm underwater. I should feel panicked in these murky depths, but I don't. My dark hair swirls around my face and tickles my shoulders. My body is weightless but strong. Every movement propels me through the cool water, twirling and turning. I kick, and my body lurches forward at a shocking speed, forcing my arms down to my sides. My fingers graze the top of my legs. They feel strange. I look down and see shimmering scales leading to an enormous fan-shaped tail. *My* tail.

I wake to intense aching in my legs. I'm on my bed in Mom's room. Someone has covered me in the crocheted throw from the end of my bed. It's dark. I must have dozed off after Claire left. A cool breeze whispers through the open crack in the window. Muffled voices from downstairs mingle with the rustle of the leaves outside. I push through the pain in my legs, stand,

and wrap the warm blanket around my shoulders. Downstairs, the reception is still lively. A crowd of faces that are vaguely familiar from earlier in the day greet me in the living room. A few of them look and nod in my direction, but their heated conversation continues as I walk toward the kitchen.

"I say this is enough now," says a voice from the couch. "We gotta show 'em who's boss here. Take back our town." The words are slurred a bit.

"It's *our* turn to hunt *them*!" A gruff voice from the corner.

"We're a fishing town after all. Let's fish!"

"We'll do it for Mark."

"For Mark."

"It's time."

I linger to try to make out more of what the voices in the living room are saying, but their battle cries are interrupted by Mom's voice. She's shouting.

From where I stand, I can see a corner of the kitchen. Gran is leaning against the counter, and Mom is facing her with her back to me. She sobs. "It's too much."

"I know, love. I can *see* your fear. It's smothering you. But it was so long ago. She's safe. Truly. I wish more than anything you could believe that," says Gran calmly.

Gran looks up and spots me in the doorway. The pained

expression on her face softens immediately, and she opens her arms. Mom turns to see what Gran is looking at, and I walk past her into Gran's arms. I close my eyes and bury my face in the scratchy wool of her blazer. The scent of her perfume swirling with the food smells of her kitchen clears my head of worry for a moment.

"See, Beth," Gran says to Mom over my head. "This is all that matters. We have everything we need right here. If we hang on tight to each other, our hearts will heal, I know it. Like a school of fish, right, Meranda?"

This is one of Gran's favorite expressions. Our family is like a school of fish. We swim together, with the current or against it, anticipating each other's turns and stops, protecting each other from dangers outside. Stronger and safer because we're together—figuratively speaking, I guess. I've always thought this was a funny analogy for our family, given how Mom feels about water, and because we live a whole country apart, but somehow in this place, it seems to fit just right. Except that lately, we haven't been swimming together at all. Mom and Gran have been swimming on their own, sometimes with Dad and Grampa, but not with me. I've been imprisoned somehow on the inside of the school. Protected. Shielded but unable to see what is happening around us.

I pull away from Gran. "Safe from what?" I ask. I wonder how many times I will have to ask questions like this before they let me swim with them. How many pieces of the truth will I get before I can put it all together? It's looking like I'm going to have to solve this mystery on my own—as if the people who know the answers aren't right here to tell me. She looks at me, about to say something, then Mom gasps. Her body is frozen. The color drains from her face, and I see that she is staring at my neck. I reflexively bring my hand to my throat. I forgot that I put on the gold tail necklace in the morning, hiding it under the collar of my dress.

"Is that …? Where did you …?" Mom stammers.

A pit opens up in my stomach. "I found it in my room. Your room," I whisper, turning the pendant over in my hand, wishing I could make it disappear. "I thought that …"

"You thought you could take it?" Mom asks, fuming.

"I guess I thought … I … I didn't know it was a big deal," I say. "I was going to ask you, and then I …"

She comes closer and lifts the golden tail from my neck, rubbing it between her fingers. She meets my eyes for a brief moment, and I see hers are filling with tears. Her jaw clenches, and she looks down at the pendant, her lips forming a tight line. Then, a split-second sting at the back of my neck as Mom snatches the necklace and rips it off me, breaking the chain.

I scream, but it doesn't sound like my voice in my ears. A gasping, breathless scream like a shorebird out of breath. I stare at Mom, horrified by this frantic, frenzied woman with the broken necklace dangling from her hand.

"Mom what are you doing—who *are* you?!" I shout, days of anger bursting from inside, erupting with a flood of tears. "I'm so sick of this. Sick of your lies and secrets." I scream through my sobs, pounding a crutch on the kitchen floor. "You've been treating me like a little kid, whispering and tiptoeing and 'handling' me, and it's not fair. I deserve to know what's going on. I'm a part of this family too." I want to keep screaming, to yell and stomp until I collapse. It feels so good to let it all out. Scary but good.

Mom doesn't move. Staring at the gold chain in her hand, she is silent.

Gran steps between us, facing me. She takes my hand in hers. "Meranda," she starts, but Mom gently pushes her aside.

"No, Mom," she says quietly, defeated. "I'll do this. She needs to hear it from me."

Gran nods and moves away, allowing Mom and me to be face-to-face again. I'm shaking, still so angry. She reaches to touch my neck, but I flinch and pull away.

"Meranda, honey, I'm so sorry. I can't believe I did that." She's crying now. "I'm so sorry if I hurt you, if I scared you. I was overcome with—seeing that necklace lit a fuse that's been threatening to blow up for years." She leans on the counter and picks at a Band-Aid on her finger. "It all feels so fresh here, like it happened yesterday, and it's too much. I'm reliving it every day, the terror of that day, the despair of having you taken from me."

What is she talking about?

"Mom?" I can't formulate a more specific question than that. I'm afraid of what I'm about to hear. "Gran?" I look to her for help.

Gran looks at her daughter, in pieces and desperate. Mom nods slowly.

"The ferry accident," Gran starts for Mom.

"Yes," Mom stands up straighter, gaining strength from her mother. "That night, August 19, 2010, was the darkest day of my life. You were three years old. We were coming home from Halkirk. You and I had just had the loveliest weekend with friends of mine from school. It was a rare warm night, and I can still see you playing on the deck of the ferry in your sundress. I had tried to get a sweater on you, but you would have none of it." She smiles, lost in a brief, precious memory, then it passes. "The wind came out of nowhere and the waves ..." She chokes on the words, then goes on. "The waves covered the ferry. I grabbed your arm and wrapped you up in my arms as tight as I could. The captain was ringing the bell, trying to direct us to the lifeboats, but the boat was tossing so much we could barely stand up, let alone make it to the other side of the deck. The next thing I knew, we were in the water. I had you. Then …" She looks at Gran, tears escaping her eyes. Then her eyes meet mine again. "She grabbed you."

"What? Who grabbed me?"

"The mermaid."

The *what*? I drop down onto the chair beside me, not trusting my aching legs to hold me up when my head is spinning. What is she saying?

Mom sits to face me. "She grabbed you. Ripped you from my arms. I pulled you back as hard as I could, but I wasn't strong enough to fight her off. She took you from me and swam away." She lowers her head into her hands, her shoulders racked with sobs.

Gran goes to Mom and puts her arms around her. Mom leans in, accepting the support.

"Your mother was hysterical when they brought her to shore," Gran continues the story. "Some of the crew had managed to free up a lifeboat before the ferry sank. They rescued everyone they could. Alex said your mother refused to be taken on board.

Not without you. They had to drag her up, exhausted. I'll never forget the look on her face when we met her on the pier. She was moving and breathing, but she looked dead. She didn't speak for days."

I can picture that woman, not that different from the one in front of me now. Shriveled, wilted, and pale. Not the mother I have known my whole life.

"The whole town searched for survivors that night," Gran says. "Near suicide in that storm, but that's what fishermen do. It was Mark that found you. He heard you laughing. When he got to you, you were surrounded by mermaids. Safe and happy. He says they wouldn't let him near you at first. They howled and thrashed at him. But when they saw his necklace, the McKenzie symbol, they quieted down and let him bring you back to us."

Gran moves her hand from her shoulder and strokes Mom's curls, old worries about her daughter mixing with new ones. My mouth gapes open.

"It was days later before your mom was able to tell us what had happened with the mermaid. Mark had thought that the mermaids were protecting you. That they'd saved you. But …"

"They *stole* you," Mom interjects. "Steven had been killed two years before and then this. They are dangerous, vicious, and evil." She wipes her cheeks with the back of her hand and stands straighter. “So we left. I couldn’t stand to be here anymore, to see the statues, the craft shops, hear the legends.” She slams her palms on the counter. “And clearly, we should not have come back. I won’t let them hurt you, Meranda. I won’t.”

I try to stand up, but my legs start to buckle, and the weight of my body on my crutches is enormous. I want to run out of the room, run from the crazy things my mother is telling me. But my throbbing legs won’t let me. So I fall back into the chair, exhausted by my family’s lies and not sure what to believe anymore. Mom and Gran are quiet, watching me. I was kidnapped by mermaids, they say. That’s how I survived the ferry sinking. The Mer-girl: taken by merfolk.

Chapter 22

Dad and I sit on the deck, staring at the French toast and bacon on our plates. Everyone else is still in bed. I heard Dad trying to sneak past my slightly opened door this morning and decided to give up on sleep. I don't know if I slept at all. I couldn't turn my brain off. In one way, learning about the ferry disaster explained so many things about my family: why we left, why we never come back, Mom's fear of water (or fear of me being around it), Mom and Dad's overprotectiveness. But somehow, I feel even more unsettled. Now there's more. Mermaids. Evil, baby-snatching, uncle-murdering mermaids. It's like my whole world has turned upside down. Or Mom has been clinging to a hallucination for the last eight years and has finally lost it? Neither option seems good for me.

While Dad was making breakfast, I had told him about the night before. Now we sit in silence outside. That's one of the best things about Dad. He is perfectly okay with sitting and listening to me without needing to present any solutions to my problems. He's got a quiet strength that sometimes goes unnoticed but can then make all the difference. On this peaceful fall morning, he is my favorite place. When he looks up, he pushes his plate aside, gulps down the last sip of his coffee, and gets up from the table.

"Let's go for a walk," he says. "Grab your shoes and a sweater."

I do as I'm told and meet him back on the deck. He leads me across the lawn toward the stairs that go down to the dock. I wish I had put on socks. The grass is wet, and in some places, crispy with frost. My bare toes burn a bit as the cold seeps through my thin canvas sneakers. The lake is still and reflects the warm pink glow that is beginning to crawl across the sky.

When we get to the top of the stairs, I stop. More like I freeze. I've been trained my whole life to be afraid of the water for all the reasons Mom can list, yet I've always felt such a pull toward it. Maybe a kind of rebellion or an exertion of independence, who knows. But now, the idea of angry, violent creatures beneath the surface makes my body recoil and want to run.

"Coming?" Dad asks.

"You sure it's safe?" I ask.

He tilts his head for a moment. "Ah, mermaids?"

"Maybe," I answer.

"I've gotcha," he says and takes my hand. "No selkie is any match for your dad." He winks and makes a goofy face.

We take the stairs to the dock, but instead of walking out over the water, Dad leads me back toward shore. At the shoreline, I notice a trail leading into the woods that must encircle the lake. We take it. We walk single file in silence, my eyes straining to avoid roots and rocks in the pale morning light. The trail is just wide enough for my crutches and they sink ever so slightly into the soft dirt and fallen leaves.

"Here." Dad stops and looks up. "This is it."

"This is what?"

"Our house."

At that very moment, the sun pokes over the hill across the lake. The reflection on the water is like someone flipped on the light switch for morning. I follow Dad's eyes and see a set of steps leading up to a pretty little house with white siding and blue shutters.

"This is where the three of us lived before we moved out West."

He walks out onto a small dock attached to the sloped yard and sits on the damp wood, his back to the water, looking up at the house. I go over and sit next to him.

"You see, Meranda? This was Mom's happiest place in the

world. This town, this lake, these people. This was home in every sense of the word. We were going to build the most incredible life here …" His words trail off and then he clears his throat. "Don't get me wrong, we love our life in Calgary. We love our life with you. You are everything to us, you get that, right? Everything. We waited for you for so long and for a time, we thought you'd never come. That night, the night of the accident, when we …" His voice cracks. "When we lost you—there are no words to describe how painful that was. How helpless we felt. Mom has never forgiven herself for losing her grip on you." He hugs his knees to his chest and stares at the white house in front of us like he's watching the scene unfold again. "I didn't think we'd ever come back from that, ever feel whole again. But then we found you." He turns to me.

"With the mermaids." I finish for him.

Dad sighs and turns to look out over the lake. "Honestly, Meranda, I know Mom is so clear about what happened, what she saw, but trauma can affect the chemicals in the brain and alter perceptions and memories. Your grandmother believes the mermaid was trying to save you. That it did save you. The McKenzie mermaid myth goes deep, and she can't let it go. I'm not sure we'll ever be able to fill in all the pieces of this story, but all that really matters is that you lived. That you're here."

I'm here. I lived.

"Do you believe in mermaids, Dad?"

There is a splash a few feet from the edge of the dock. The sound jolts Dad to his feet in a panic, and he scans the surface of the water.

"What is it?" I roll my body to the side and reach for my crutches. I'm pulling myself up when I hear the splash again. Closer this time. When I look up, all that remain are rings of ripples near the shoreline.

Dad's eyes are wide. His hands are shaking as he helps me to my feet and back onto the trail.

"Selkies?" I ask him, locking his eyes with mine.

He laughs nervously. "Naaaw, more like a porpoise or lost harbor seal." But the fear on his face says differently. "We should get back. Mom will be wondering where we are."

The walk back to the house is quicker than our walk out this morning. The light makes it much easier for me to navigate the small obstacles and unevenness on the trail, but the biggest difference is the pace. Dad is practically jogging ahead of me. My forearms burn from the extra pressure I'm putting on my crutches with the rocky terrain, but I'm used to swallowing a bit of discomfort so as not to be left behind.

When the trail pops out at Gran and Grampa's dock, Dad is

waiting for me. My glasses have steamed up with the heat from my face in the cool fall air. I stop to take them off and dry them on the sleeve of my sweater and to catch my breath.

"Sorry, kid, I guess I was going a bit fast, eh? Here, let me give you a hand up the steps." He takes my arm and gives me a boost, all the while looking behind him at the lake.

"It's all okay, it's all fine," he says, more to himself than to me.

And with that, I have my answer. Can it really be possible? My logical, fact-loving scientist dad believes in mermaids. I have no clue what to do with that. And the worst part is, he's clearly afraid.

Chapter 23

When we get back to the house, Gran is in the kitchen cleaning up from last night. "Good morning, you two," she says turning around from the sink. "Where'd you get off to so early?"

"Dad took me out to show me our old house," I tell her.

She and Dad exchange looks, and she says, "Oh, how lovely. Isn't it a sweet little place? I often wonder how things would have turned out if you'd all lived next door. Wishful thinking for a gran, right?" She smiles at me and wipes her wet hands on her apron.

She cups my cheeks in her damp hands for a second, then kisses me on the forehead. "You okay this morning, sweetie? I know last night was hard."

"I've never seen Mom like that before." My mom may worry about my safety, but she is always in charge, sure, strong. The boss. This place is making her seem small and lost, more with each passing day. She's like a stranger. It hits me that I'm homesick. I want to go back to where our family is normal, where Mom always knows what to do, where there are no secrets. When Mom and I are a team, facing life together. But that place doesn't really exist anymore. The secrets were there all along, I just hadn't known.

We all jump when the phone rings.

Gran answers. "Oh, hi, love. Yep, she's right here. It's for you, Meranda. It's Claire."

"Hey," I say after grabbing the phone.

"Up for more detective work?" Claire asks. She's excited. "I have an idea. Let's hit the *Gazette* office and see what we can dig up. You in?"

"Uh, sure," I answer, aware of Dad's and Gran's eyes and ears on me. "My dad's standing right beside me. Let me see if he can drive me?"

"Oooh, good point," Claire says, getting my meaning. "Top secret, right? Okay, how about you get him to drop you at my grandparents' place? We can walk from here."

Dad and Gran practically fight over who will drive me into town—Dad wins by a hair. I think they're happy I've got a friend. Or happy to have me out of the house. Doesn't matter. To be honest, I kind of need to get out of here for a while too.

Claire is sitting on the front steps when we pull up. Her red hair is pulled back in a messy bun, and she's wearing a huge knit scarf that covers half her face.

"How about I come get you gals around noon, and we'll hit the Chowder House one more time before we go back West?" Dad says.

"Sounds good. Thanks for the ride."

"No problem, kiddo. Have fun, be caref—" He catches himself. "Have fun."

I lean over and kiss him on the cheek, then I'm out the passenger door, rushing up the steps. "So we have to make sure we're back before noon," I say as I watch him drive away. "My dad will be here by then and will freak out if we're not around." A twinge in my conscience makes me hesitate for a second. I don't lie to my parents. But desperate times call for desperate measures. And let's face it, they've been lying to me for years. Besides, they're so wrapped up in their own stuff, I bet they'll even forget I'm gone.

"Sure." Claire unwraps herself a bit and smiles. It's an empty smile.

"What's wrong?"

"It's dumb." Claire covers her face again with the scarf. "Mom called last night. I could hear Grandma talking to her in the kitchen, and I waited. But she didn't want to talk to me."

"That can't be right," I say. "She's your mom, of course she did. Maybe you just heard wrong." But I can see from Claire's face that's not the case. "What did you say?"

"To who?" Claire looks confused.

"Your grandma. Did you ask her about it?"

Claire laughs. "No way. Everyone always starts crying when I ask about Mom. It's kinda awful."

"You've got to tell them how you feel," I say. The look from Claire is like a slap in the face. Right. I should talk. Me, the girl who has been silently screaming inside since we arrived. Then, as if we're struck by the absurdity at the same time, we both laugh out loud. It feels so good, loosening the knots tied in my stomach. "Okay," I wipe a tear of laughter from my eye. "Point taken. But secrets can't be good for anyone, right? Me included." I pause, take a deep breath. "I had it out with my mom last night. She finally told me about the ferry accident—and, well … they all think I was rescued—or stolen, depending on who you believe—by *mermaids*." I wait for Claire to retort with sarcasm or disbelief. She doesn't. She just lets me talk. "I feel like there's more to all this than anyone's telling me. Why else would my entire family, including my grandparents, have hidden this from me?"

Claire raises her eyebrows and gives a shrug. "Well, let's

go find out for ourselves, then." She stands up and gives my shoulder a squeeze as we head out to the sidewalk. It's not far, just a few blocks to the newspaper office. "You sure you're okay to walk?" she asks, looking at my legs.

The expression on my face must have been enough of an answer. "Sorry," she says. We keep going.

The *Gazette* office is an old building the shape of a cereal box, with red wooden shingles that are peeling enough to expose flecks of old white paint underneath. From the street, it looks like it's sparkling in the sun, but up close it just looks rundown. The bell above the door announces our entrance, and a boy about our age gets up from behind the pine countertop.

"Hey, Drew, is your uncle around?" Claire asks. She's holding her head high and standing taller than she was a minute ago.

"Uh, hey, Claire. He's in the back—what do you need?" he answers.

"Just need to talk to him a minute. Can we go back? This is Meranda by the way." She lifts the countertop and starts walking to the back of the office without waiting for an answer.

I follow Claire through the obstacle course of desks toward the back of the room. Before she knocks, she says, "Drew's in my class. His uncle Howard runs the paper."

"It's open!" shouts a voice.

Claire begins to open the door, but it gets stuck halfway, blocked by mountains of newspapers.

"Sorry, working my way through the piles … squeeze yourselves around!" I still can't see the face emitting that voice, but we do as we're told and stumble into the tiny windowless office. I pass Claire my crutches to tuck my body through the narrow space and steady myself when I grab them on the other side. Now I see the speaker—an older man sitting at the desk. He's a bit hunched and it looks like he's been sitting in that chair for years.

"Hi, Mr. McKeller. This is Meranda, Gwenn Campbell's granddaughter, from Calgary."

"Ah, hello, Meranda. Well, my word. The miracle baby. Home at last? So sorry about Mark. He was a good one." Howard McKeller starts to stand up to offer a handshake, but his body seems to take too long to obey so he gives up and plops back in the chair with a huff.

"What can I do for you, Claire?"

"Meranda just found out about the ferry accident and the whole miracle baby thing. With that and the legends and all the talk about Mark's death, she, or we, had some questions. About the accident and well … about the …" Claire hesitates.

Howard clears his throat. "About the mermaids," he whispers.

I take a deep breath. "Are they real?" I ask the obvious question, not sure what I hope he will say.

Howard closes his eyes for a moment, then looks up at me, his blue eyes framed by years of smiles. "Of course they are."

I sigh, the air rushing from my chest like a deflating balloon. I feel like I've been holding my breath for days, and now this man has released it by simply answering a direct question. I realize that I have wanted to believe—that Mom isn't crazy, that my family isn't coming apart over a silly legend, that mermaids could be real.

He leans over with a groan and opens the bottom drawer of the filing cabinet beside his desk. With another groan, he pulls out a leather binder and places it on the desk, open so we can see. The yellowed sheet of paper has the typewritten title "Fraser Baby Saved by Mermaids," and the date in the corner is June 4, 1973. I slide the binder toward me and flip through the pages. More yellowed sheets of paper, all in plastic page protectors, all with stories of mermaids. "Selkies Bring Luck to Local Fishing Industry," "Number of Merfolk in Pod Up This Year," "Crew Saved from Storm by Pod of Mermaids." Then, the headlines on the less yellowed paper: "Vessels Destroyed While Docked in Harbour," "Mermaids Sabotage Fishing Nets," "Mermaids Attack Local Ferry, 20 Lost."

"What are these?" I ask.

"Newspaper articles, of course," Howard says. "*Gazette* articles."

"But these are not newspapers," I say. "They're stories typed on paper."

Howard smiles slowly. He's waiting for me to figure this out on my own, but I can't. Eventually he answers. "Can't publish this stuff, y'know? We'd either look delusional or our town would be overrun with tourists, scientists, and conspiracy theorists. Neither are very good options, right? We write it 'cause it's news, and it's the truth, but we write it for ourselves, no one else. I've been keeping this archive of the mermaids of Skye for fifty years. To document our story."

There are photos in the binder as well. Most of them are black and white. Many are the same grainy photos I saw in Claire's grandmother's book. Shadowy images of the lake, some with outlines of tails, others, like the one on the cover of the book, look like people waist-deep in the middle of the water, as if they are standing in a shallow pond. They are all taken from far away and remind me of the photos we saw of the Loch Ness monster when we visited Scotland.

Howard takes the binder from me and flips to a page near the end. It's a sketch in pencil, a swirly tail inside a circle. I recognize it immediately. It's the pendant.

"I know this symbol," I say. "I've seen it, but I don't know what it means."

"This is the McKenzie symbol," Howard says. "*Dìon maighdeann-mhara.* They all have one. Used to wear 'em all the time."

Mermaid's protection. That's why Mom lost her mind when she saw me wearing it. Did Gran still have hers? Did she stop wearing it after the ferry accident?

As I absently flip through the "articles," my breath catches in my chest when I see a familiar face. Mom. The headline reads "Miracle Baby Rescued by Mermaids" and below it is a photo of Mom holding a toddler. Me. It's one of the family photos we have hanging in our hallway at home. I read the page out loud.

"'Three-year-old Meranda Morgan was found late last night on the shores of Bras d'Or Lake by her great-uncle Mark McKenzie, following an extensive over-water search. The child had been presumed drowned when she went missing during the sinking of the Skye–Halkirk Ferry the day before. "She was crawling in the sand on the beach," says McKenzie. "I heard her giggling. Fit as a fiddle she was. It's a miracle." Miracle? Or mermaid rescue—'"

Drew rushes in through the office door, flushed and breathless. "Uncle Howard. Better come quick." He bends over, gulping in air. "It's the mermaids—they're in trouble."

Chapter 24

We follow Drew and Howard out the door of the *Gazette* office onto the sidewalk. Across the street, several trucks are parked, and more are pulling up. Dozens of people are milling about on the pier and talking in angry tones. A white truck roars up, and three people get out. I recognize two of them as Jeffrey and Kate, Uncle Mark's crewmates. Jeffrey opens the truck bed and takes out what looks like a shotgun and two large nets. The crowd separates, and people begin boarding three of the fishing boats moored by the pier, carrying the gear that was unloaded.

"What in the name of heaven ...?" Howard puts his hands on the top of his head, baffled and worried.

I remember the vengeful discussions I overheard at the funeral reception. "They're hunting. Or fishing. For mermaids," I say. "To avenge Mark." My heart sinks as I say it.

“No.” The color drains from Howard’s face.

We stand and watch the vessels leave. Shouts from the men and women aboard echo off the water and fade into the evening sky. I don’t know what to think or feel. So many questions. How are these grown men and women, experienced fishermen, heading out on a mermaid hunt? It sounds ridiculous, but it certainly feels real watching the activity in front of us. I feel sick. The words from the newspaper article are burned inside my eyes, imprinted on top of everything I’m seeing right now. “Miracle? Or mermaid rescue.” Rescue or kidnapping, I wonder. And anyway, why did the mermaid take me? Of all the people on that boat, including Mom, a McKenzie, why *me*?

“I’ll get the camera.” Drew and Howard disappear back into the newspaper office, and Claire and I are left, stunned, on the sidewalk by ourselves. Alone, like two pebbles in a raging stream, trying not to get pulled along with the current. The mermaid on the front of Gus’s tour boat bobs in the waves, pointing out at the fleet approaching the horizon as though warning her friends.

Claire shakes her head. “You’ve got to be kidding me. These are seasoned Maritimers, hunting mermaids. Ridiculous, right? Or embarrassing—I can’t decide.”

“Right,” I say. But I’m not so sure. The pit in my stomach fills with worry. Fear. I realize I'm afraid for the mermaids; if they *are* real, I don't want them to be hurt. I see Mom's pained expression in my mind, her hatred for the creatures that stole her baby—stole me. I feel guilty, like I'm betraying her for wanting to protect them. But the pull to the mermaids and to the water is so strong. Like an instinct.

"What about Gus's boat?" Claire asks, pulling me from my deeply confusing string of thoughts.

"What about it?"

"Do you think a mermaid tour boat could have any clues about mermaids? Gus is the only man alive who claims to have actually *seen* one. Or maybe we can find some proof he's made the whole thing up?"

Of course. Gus. Why didn't we think of him earlier? "Right," I say to Claire. "We should talk to Gus."

Claire is off running. "Talk? No way!" she yells back. "Not to that creep!" I start to follow her toward the pier. Toward the water. She stops for a second in front of Gus's boat, then climbs over the edge and disappears aboard. My sweaty palms slip on the metal handles of my crutches and one clangs to the ground. I bend to pick it up, feeling my heart pounding in my throat, and when I stand back up, my heart skips a beat. Gus is on the pier. Walking toward his boat, carrying what looks like a spear gun and a net. I strain to see Claire. I think I can make out the top of her red head in the cab of the boat, and I wave my crutch in the air frantically, trying to warn her. Nothing. I move as fast as I can toward the boat and Gus, unsure of exactly what I will do when I get there. Suddenly, Gus stops walking. He pats his back pockets, then his front, lowers his head in exasperation, and turns back to his car. I freeze beside a streetlight. Luckily, he is too focused on his task to notice me there. As he opens the passenger door and ducks inside, digging for something, I take the opportunity to race toward the boat. I grab the edge and lean over.

"Claire!" A loud whisper. "Claire! We gotta go!"

I see her now, in the window of the cab. She meets my eyes, and her expression reflects my fear. I turn to see Gus start to back out of the front seat, keys jingling in his hand. What do I do? I can hear my mother's voice clanging in my brain. She'll flip if she finds out that I hopped into a boat by the pier. Forget that I lied to them about where I was going today. But I remind myself of their secrets. This is my story. And I deserve to know the whole truth.

I can tell that Claire's not the type to be easily spooked, but she looks terrified right now. I roll my body into the boat. I can't leave Claire alone here. I stay low on the deck so as not to be seen and crawl, crutches dragging behind me, to meet her in the cab. We duck down into the corner, under the navigation table. There are mermaids everywhere. Posters on the walls, stickers on the windows, and even a dancing mermaid bobblehead near the steering wheel. The figure is nodding and gyrating as the vessel bobs in the waves.

Thud. Boots on board. He's here. Gus's heavy footsteps drag back and forth across the deck. He grunts, hauling something behind him, occasionally cursing under his breath. A motor starts. We've got to get off *now*. I peer out the glass facing the back of the boat. Gus has his back to us, struggling with some rope. I wave Claire over, getting ready to escape without being noticed. My hands are in my crutches, Claire's are on the door handle.

I double-check Gus's position and steady my legs on the rocking floor. "One, two, three," I whisper. "Now!" Claire bursts out the door, and I follow close behind. On my feet, steady, with my crutches firmly planted. But Claire stops cold, and I crash into her from behind. It takes me only a moment to see why. We're no longer moored at the pier. The boat is floating at least three hundred feet from shore. We're trapped.

Chapter 25

"What the—?" Gus hears our commotion and whips around to see us clinging to the railing of the boat. "How'd you two get on here?"

Claire thinks faster than I do. "Hi, Mr. MacDonald. We're so sorry. We were goofing around and didn't hear you come on board. Meranda was admiring the mermaid on the bow, and I just thought ... it was a stupid idea. I'm sorry." Claire stops talking when Gus makes his way up the length of the boat to where we're standing. He's swaying, even more than he should in the wavy conditions. When he gets a bit closer, I can smell why: he's been drinking. He blinks slowly and looks us both up and down.

"McKenzie girl, right?" he says, eyeing my crutches.

"Actually, it's Morgan," I correct him. "Meranda Morgan. We met at the wake."

"Damn McKenzies," he continues, ignoring me. He stumbles

over his words, gripping the railing outside the cab for balance. "Y'd all be better off if you just left the rest of us alone. You're no better than us. You'd have done the same … meddling fool. Not so high and mighty now, eh?" he trails off, mumbling more to himself than to us.

"If you could just bring us back to the pier, sir, we'll be out of your way. Again, we're so sorry to have trespassed." He snaps back to us at the sound of Claire's voice, looks toward the pier, and shakes his head in frustration. "Fine," he says. He goes into the cab and starts the motor, turning the boat around toward town. It's facing into the wind now, and the waves swell bigger. Tossing in the rough water, the vessel suddenly feels so small. A flash lights up the navy sky, and I see alarm in Claire's eyes. Even Gus looks worried. He runs his hands through his greasy hair and rubs his red eyes, trying hard to focus on his destination. As a crack of thunder shakes the cab, Gus's white knuckles tighten on the wheel.

"It's all right, Claire," I say, steadying my trembling voice as best I can. "Gus is one of Skye's best sailors. Uncle Mark always used to say so. Used to say, 'There's no storm that man can't weather.' I'm sure this is nothing for him, right, sir? I know you're scared, but Gus has got this. Old pro, right, Gus?"

Gus blinks slowly and nods. His bleary eyes focus firmly

on my face, and I pray that my lies will overpower the alcohol in his body long enough to get us back to shore. It seems to be working, so I continue. "Uncle Mark talked about you a lot. In fact, even on the night he died, before leaving, he—" Gus's expression darkens. He shakes his head, and a menacing smile slowly forms across his face. I panic. What have I said? My desperate attempt to talk him down went too far, and somehow I've made things worse.

"I wondered," he says. "Swore he hadn't told anyone. *Swore* it. But you McKenzies always stick together, everyone else be damned. The whole clan know, then? Stringing me along now?" He's paranoid. But about what? He leans on the controls, his hands now off the wheel. The boat is rocking wildly, and I can barely keep myself upright. I look to Claire. Her wide eyes tell me she has no idea what he's talking about either.

I try again. Willing myself to sound calm. "Nah, Gus. No one told anyone anything. My family sure as heck never tells *me* anything. I know less about my family than you do, I'm sure. No one is more clueless than me."

I can tell Gus isn't convinced. "Too late for that now, girl. No backtracking. Is that what you gals were reading 'bout in the library? Yeah, me wife told me yous were there." He's coming toward me. "I tried to spook yas that day—to scare you to stay away. You're all the same. Mark didn't know when to keep his nose outta other folks' business either. Looks like it's a family trait. He shoulda left it alone but no. Had to call me out. Said he was gonna make things right for Steven." Steven? What is he talking about? "Now I s'pose they've sent you to prove me guilty."

My mind is racing, trying to piece this drunken man's tirade together. "Sent me? No one sent me. Are you crazy? Who would send me, the kid with legs that don't work, to do anything?" I wave my right crutch at him to emphasize my point. The move startles him, and he lunges for me, causing the crutch to slip from my hand. A wave crashes into the boat at that moment and thrusts us to the opposite side of the cab. I fall to the floor and slide just out of his reach. But where's Claire? Did she fall? I grab a handle on the wall by the door to pull myself up and see her fumbling with a rope near the back of the boat. She waves her arms to get my attention, and I see that she is standing next to a dinghy, untying it. My feelings shift from relief that Claire's all right to gratitude that she's found us a way out to terror that the way out is a tiny boat on a stormy lake.

A hand on my leg, pulling me down. Gus is yelling over the waves. "I'm so sorry." He's crying. "It was an accident, a horrible accident, and I was a coward. I am a coward." I try to pull my leg back, but my stiff muscles don't obey. He's got me.

"Meranda!" Claire's voice reaches me. "Now!"

Without a thought, I jam my crutch into Gus's hand. He yelps and slides backward along the floor when another wave slams the side of the boat. I'm up for a moment, then I'm knocked down when the craft is lifted by another wave. Crawling may be faster anyway. I make my way across the deck, which is still relatively dry, to Claire, who is waiting, holding the rope to the dinghy. She lowers it into the water and leans down to keep it steady. "You first," she yells.

I've never been on a boat before—not since the ferry, apparently. I think of Mom as I lower myself into the tiny, flimsy vessel bouncing on the waves like a child's toy. She'd absolutely freak out. Me in a dinghy in a storm.

"I'm in," I call.

Claire turns to untie the final knot to release us, but Gus is there, stopping her, his hand on hers. She yanks her hand away as a wave tips the boat to the side, and Gus is thrown back, disappearing from sight. Claire grips the rope and manages to stay on her feet until the boat lurches again. The front is lifted onto a massive wave, throwing it almost vertically, and Claire is flung into the air, over my head. I see her disappear under the waves.

"Claire!" I scream.

I'm frantic, scanning the water for my friend. I see a flash of red hair a few feet away, then arms splashing. Desperate, I grab a life jacket from the floor of the dinghy and take a split second to decide what to do. The dinghy is still tied to Gus's boat, and I can't reach the rope from here to free myself. Claire will surely drown without help. I hear Mom's voice in my mind: "I just worry that your legs won't be strong enough to keep your head above water." But I see other words again behind my eyes: "Mermaid rescue." When I look down, I see my island-shaped birthmark bright red against my cold bluish skin. Maybe this is where all the secrets lead. Where did I really come from? The only child who looks nothing like her parents. The precious child never allowed to dip her toes in the ocean. The frail child with aching legs. Is that why the mermaids came for me? To take me back where I belong? Could it be?

But there's no time for this—the only thing I'm absolutely sure of is that I can't leave Claire out there a moment longer. I have to try. I take a breath, weave my arms through the life jacket, stand up as best I can, and jump. Every bit of my body stings as it hits the frigid water, like an icy fire is consuming me. For a moment, all my muscles freeze, like my legs do when they're tired, and I'm sinking. I flap my arms and am able to get my head to the surface. Frantically, I gasp for air as my chest stiffens, and my face is pelted with icy raindrops. I hear a scream. Was that someone calling my name? I try yelling in reply but am smothered by another wave. My legs, burning a few seconds ago, are now numb and heavy. The sensation seems to be climbing up from my toes like I'm being swallowed up. I'm sinking. Helpless. Drowning. Dark.

Malcolm McKenzie was certain his memories were sound. What the doctors called delusions, distortions of memory resulting from his traumatic experience, remained consistent and clear until the day that he died. In one of his final interviews, he stated, "I woke up with sand in me mouth. At first, I wasn't sure if it was just the roughness of my dry mouth, but it was indeed sand. My stomach was tossin' like the ship in the storm the night before, and I rolled over to heave and that's when I saw her. At the edge of the water, an arm's length away.

"She was so beautiful, I recall fighting the urge to be sick right there on the sand so as not to embarrass m'self in front of such a beauty. I tried to right m'self but found I couldn't even sit up, so I rolled to see her more clearly and couldn't believe me eyes. She was a selkie. With a tail that shimmered and glowed in the sun, more spectacular than a sunset on the waves. I realized then that she had saved me from the wreck. I tried to thank her, to ask her name, where we were, but found I had no voice. She nodded, smiled, and slid backward into the lake. Then she was gone, like the most heavenly dream."

Legends of the Lakes **by Sarah Chapman, 2010**

Chapter 26

Everything hurts. I try to roll over, but my body is heavy, and my arms are tied down. I hear beeping in the distance and a whisper in my ear as the darkness washes over me and sweeps me away.

More beeping. Voices. This time louder than whispers. I hear my name being called as if from another shore. I inhale to shout back, but no sound emerges. I fight to open my eyes, but my eyelids won't obey. Black.

"Meranda, I'm here … Can you hear me?"

I struggle to pull myself to the surface, to will my mind clear and push through the murkiness surrounding me.

"Meranda …?"

It's my mother's voice. Only muffled and thick. Far away.

"Don't try to talk. Everything's going to be all right. You're safe now."

More beeping, machines, bright lights. Then back underwater.

Chapter 27

"We should never have brought her back here. I don't know what I was thinking. This is all my fault—every bit of it." Mom's voice.

"Honey, this has been eating you up for years. The truth needed to come out sometime. Maybe this is all for the best … or will be in the end." Gran.

"For the best? My baby is lying in a hospital bed. She nearly drowned! It's happening all over again." Sobs.

"Beth, this is *not* the same. You need to calm down. Breathe. You've been holding on so tight to this secret for so long that it's blinding you to the truth. The real truth. Can't you see what's been happening this week? The secrecy has been pushing Meranda away. I know you're trying to protect her, but can't you see how you will lose her this way? You need to let her break out of the shell you've built around her. Let life touch her a little."

"But Mom, I …" Mom's words disappear. Drowned by more sobs.

My throat starts to tickle. I try to swallow so as not to interrupt the most honest words I've heard since we left Calgary. I want to be invisible. Want Mom and Gran to forget I'm here. But I'm still not sure where here is. I'm in a bed, with very scratchy sheets. The air smells like chemicals, and there is a humming sound in my ear. Then beeping. I hear feet on the floor.

"It's her heart rate. It's climbing." Mom is beside me now. "Meranda? Can you hear me?"

A cough explodes from my throat, then another and another.

"It's all right, sweetie, you're safe. I'm here. Take slow breaths." Mom's hand on my shoulder. "Can you open your eyes?"

I try. They're stuck. And I can barely get enough air into my lungs.

"Okay, one step at a time." Mom's breath is warm on my face. "Slow, deep breaths." Now her cheek on mine. She's holding me close. "I've got you."

The wave of panic recedes. I'm all right. Mom's here. I'm all right. Slowly, air reaches my lungs. Then again. And again. I'm breathing. Then I'm able to open my eyes. I recognize the blurred shape in front of me as my mother, but the other fuzzy blobs in the room are unfamiliar. This is not my room, not at home or at Gran and Grampa's. Mom's warm hands graze my cheek as she puts my glasses on my face.

"There you are. I'm so glad you're back." All I see are her blue eyes as she presses her forehead on mine. In spite of everything that's happened between us, Mom can still make everything okay.

"Mom?" My voice croaks. "What ...? Where ...?"

"You're in the hospital, Meranda. There was an accident. But you're okay. You're going to be just fine."

I sit up. The beeping starts again, and Mom gets up and pushes a button on the monitor screen above me. I see Gran sitting on a couch under the window. When I smile at her, she dabs her eyes with a tissue, then comes to my bedside and takes my hand.

"You gave us a scare, m'love," she says.

"I did? What happened?" I reach back in my mind. The water. The darkness. Was that a dream?

A nurse enters my room. "Look who's awake," she says to me. Then to Mom, "Beth, we've got the transport arranged for tomorrow morning. You'll all be home by suppertime." She rubs Mom's arm, pats my feet under the covers, and then leaves the room.

"Home?" I ask.

"Home," Mom answers. "They were going to transfer you to the children's hospital in Halifax, but I've managed to get us sent back to Calgary instead. It'll be good to get home."

I look over at Gran. She closes her eyes and shakes her head. Her shoulders slump a bit.

"It's for the best," Mom says. "It's best for everyone." She looks at Gran firmly as she says this. I can tell Gran does not agree, but I don't know why. It probably has something to do with their conversation that I overheard a few minutes ago. About the truth. The truth about what happened? I go back into my mind again. The water. The waves … The boat … Claire.

"Claire!" I shout. "Where is she? I don't remember …" Mom and Gran both look up in surprise. "She was in the water. We were trapped. I jumped." My heart races as the memories come flooding back to me.

"She's all right, Meranda. Swallowed a bit of water, but she's going to be just fine." Mom sits down next to me and rubs my leg on top of the hospital sheet. "What else do you remember?" She is speaking so slowly and deliberately that I know something important has happened.

"Gus MacDonald," I blurt. "He was on the boat. He'd been drinking, and he started going on about Uncle Mark and the

McKenzies and Steven Kirkland. I didn't understand it all, but he was scared. Then the storm ..."

"Yes, Jeffrey and Kate and the rest of the crew found him last night," Gran says with a grimace. "His boat was drifting, and they towed him to shore. He was a mess. He thought he'd killed you girls, was blubbering and going on about his heavy soul. Serves him right."

I look to Mom. She gives me a pained look and explains. "He confessed on the spot. Turns out Steven had caught him stealing from his company all those years ago and confronted him one night. They argued and fought on deck, and Steven got caught in the hooks and rigging ... Pulled overboard. Gus panicked and told everyone a mermaid had attacked Steven and dragged him under."

I can't believe this. After all these years. "He made it up?"

Gran nods curtly. "Completely. And was able to turn it into a little business venture for himself too. Scoundrel." She starts pacing. "And then—" She pauses, takes a deep breath. "Mark was going through some company financial records and found some notes Steven had made about account inconsistencies. That night he asked Gus about it. Gus told the police that when Mark confronted him, he told him everything. Claims that he was tired of carrying the guilt and that he and Mark had worked out a way for him to repay Steven's family, apologize, and finally come clean. But on the way back to shore, Mark collapsed over the side of the vessel while untangling some line and was knocked overboard by a wave. Gus said he lost his nerve and continued his lies. He's like a curse, that man." Gran stops and sits back down in her chair in the corner of the room. She drops her head in her hands. "Autopsy results confirmed it this morning. Heart attack."

"Gus is a liar and a coward for sure, but he didn't actually *kill* anyone, Gwenn." It's Dad. I'm almost surprised at how happy I am to see him. Like it's been months. "Hi, kiddo." He kisses my head and lingers for a moment, breathing me in, like he feels the same way.

"Sure as heck almost did last night, Gabe." Mom is red-faced now and angry.

"Mom, I'm all right. And we shouldn't have been there to begin with." I don't want a family fight right now. My head is pounding.

"Apparently years of guilt, combined with thinking you girls were researching him in the library and then you two being on his boat were enough for his remorse to bubble right over," Dad says. "Let's let the detectives sort the rest out, now, shall we? We have our girl here safe and sound."

Mom is rubbing her arms and rocking on her feet. She won't meet my eyes.

"All right, everyone," Gran says. "I'm going to tell you what will happen next. Beth, you will go out there and cancel the transfer to Calgary. You all need to stay here until we've had a chance to work through this—as a family. It's high time we stopped dancing around this poor child. We've been trying to protect her all these years like a precious, delicate egg, but now it's clear that we're getting in the way of her hatching into the confident, strong person that she is meant to be. Now go."

Mom's arms drop to her sides, and her jaw tightens. Without a word, she leaves the room and goes to the nursing station, presumably to do as she was just told by my bossy, fabulous grandmother.

Dad smiles. "Well said, Gwenn." He winks at Gran and me.

"Someone had to." Gran winks back.

The air in the room is lighter. I even giggle a bit at how Mom got bullied by Gran. But the giggle doesn't get rid of the sloshing worry in my gut. What else am I about to find out?

Chapter 28

In spite of my desperate efforts to keep my eyes open, my weak body is dragged down into sleep. When I open my eyes next, I notice a few bags packed by the door, and I hear Mom's voice in the hall. The orange and pink light from the sunrise bounces in from the window, creating a rainbow on the cream-colored hospital blanket. Have I slept all night?

"There you are." A red blob leans in front of my face. Claire! A wave of relief rushes through me.

I put on my glasses to find my friend sitting on a chair beside my bed. She's wearing a hospital gown too.

"What a night, right?" she says, her eyes wide.

"I'm so glad you're okay!" I tell her and reach for her hand. "I can't remember what happened after you fell into the water. I didn't know if … but you're all right?"

"Yep, a bit banged up and bruised but no permanent damage,"

she says. "I don't remember much either. Just getting thrown from the boat, not being able to keep my head above the crazy waves, then …"

"What?"

"Feeling like I was being lifted from under my arms. Then the next thing I remember is waking up in the hospital."

"Me too. I remember jumping in after you, then … here."

"Jeffrey found you girls near the beach just east of town," Dad says. I didn't even notice him on the plastic chair in the corner. "When they found Gus and he told them everything, they began the search for you two."

"You jumped in after me? Into those waves?" Claire grips my hand. "You're crazy. So *you* saved me. Saved us." She stands and throws her arms around me. "How did you have the guts to—"

"I have been wanting to ask the same thing." It's Mom. She's leaning on the doorframe. I wonder how long she's been listening. "Hi, Claire," she says, coming into the room and sitting on the other side of the bed. "Meranda, what were you thinking? What on earth made you think you could jump into the lake? In a storm?"

All the thoughts and suspicions swirling around me for the past few days are finally hitting me dead-on, like a hurricane. I can't avoid it any longer. The only way I could have survived, could have saved Claire—it's clear to me now. I'm shaking as I say, "I thought … wondered … it made sense …" I don't know how to explain. "My legs, the secrets, the miracles in the water." What will happen when I finally say this out loud? Will my life change forever? I cover my face with my hands. I don't want to meet anyone's eyes. "Am I … a mermaid?" I feel ridiculous as the words leave my mouth.

The silence in the room is more threatening than the waves last night. I'm drowning in it. Suffocating in the weight of it. I need someone to say something.

"Oh, honey." Mom's voice is next to me now. Her arm around me, her head leaning on mine. "No … you're not a mermaid," she says, taking my hand. "You're even better. You're my girl. My brave, incredible daughter."

But that's the only explanation—for all of it. There's no way Claire and I could have survived. Not with my weak legs in the storm. And all the signs point to—

"*You* saved Claire," says Dad. "You don't need a mermaid tail to account for all of this. You have everything you need—exactly as you are. Our Meranda."

"But I couldn't have." I can still taste the terror, as I clung to the life jacket, jumping into the lake, sure that we were both going to drown.

"When Jeffrey found you, you had Claire under her arms," Dad says. "The life jacket was just keeping your faces above water, and you were barely conscious. You kept yourself and Claire afloat last night. You, Meranda. *You* jumped into the storm after your friend. That move took more guts than most folks will ever have. You. As you are." He strokes my hair from my face.

I gape at them, hardly believing—but little by little, the realization trickles in, and I begin to see that what they're saying must be true. *Just me.*

"It breaks my heart that those words are surprising to you." Mom reaches for my hand. "I think my fear has gotten in the way of you knowing your true strength. All of this, all this time, has been about me, not you. *My* fear, *my* weakness, *my* lies. I'm so, so sorry. I hope you can forgive me one day."

"Forgive *us*," Dad says.

I let their words sink into me. It had felt so true, when I said it. I had *known* I was a mermaid. I had so wanted it to be real. But now I realize that what I have really wanted was to hear them say what they just did. That I am strong, that I belong. For better or for worse, my legs are just my legs, I am who I am. And for the first time, I am beginning to believe I might be okay. Or even better.

Chapter 29

After we say goodbye to Claire, Gran and Grampa pick us up in the truck to take us home.

Home. My grandparents' house. *Home.*

The late afternoon sunlight is enjoying a last dance on the lake before sunset, sending tiny flashes of light through the trees. I roll down the window to taste the air. It smells like salt and pine branches. I want to stay here, in Cape Breton, with my family. My whole family. The wind wails through the forest as we get closer to the lake. It's getting louder. No one else in the truck seems to notice.

"Shhhh," I say.

"What is it, kiddo?" Dad asks.

"Listen," I answer. "What is that?"

Grampa turns off the radio, and everyone is silent. They hear it too. Grampa pulls the truck to the side of the road and turns off the engine. A wailing sound echoes across the lake.

"Is it a bird?" Mom asks.

"Whatever it is, it sounds like it's in pain," says Gran.

"What should we do?" I ask, already knowing the answer. I unbuckle my seatbelt and open the door. "We have to help."

"Meranda, wait! Where are you going? It's not safe." We all stare at Mom as those last three words leave her lips. To my great surprise, she smiles, then laughs. A big, loud belly laugh. "So, apparently I have a short memory," she says, breathless and wiping tears from the corners of her eyes. "Sorry, sweetie. Old habits die hard. It may take me a while to loosen my grip, but I promise I'll try. Not like you solved a mystery and saved a drowning kid or anything." We all join in her laughter, relieved, as she reaches back to squeeze my shoulder. "But remember, you did just get out of the hospital, so I'm not completely out of line." She smiles at me, and I smile back. We're going to be okay.

Dad gets out of the truck and heads around to the back. "You'll be needing these, m'lady." He reaches into the truck bed and hands me the crutches the hospital gave me. Mine are gone, probably at the bottom of the lake. These ones are a bit too small but will work for now. "Mom's right, though. You may want to take it easy."

"Sure." I brush them off and start walking.

I lead the way, weaving through the trees toward the sound.

The others follow, quietly. Toward the lake. We're all unsure about the sound, curious and nervous. The sun has just dropped behind the hills, and the sky is a mix of pink and inky blue. A foggy mist creeps up from the water, blurring the edges of the forest shapes in front of me. At the water's edge, my eyes land on someone in the weeds a few feet away. I stop. Wait for the others to see it too. Mom grabs my arm, holding me back.

"Hello?" she calls.

The wailing stops, and the person startles, thrashing in the shallow water.

"Are you okay?" Mom calls.

The figure is still again, and I eventually make out the shape of a woman covered in weeds.

We all see it. My heart is pounding in my ears.

"She's stuck," I say. "She'll drown. We have to help." I run as fast as I'm able, my crutches sinking in the mud near the lake's edge. Dad is behind me.

"It's all right," I call out. "We're here to help you."

She turns and looks at us. Her dark eyes huge with terror, black hair matted around her face and down her back. Suddenly, an enormous tail emerges from the water. The scales iridescent in the evening light, glimmering with pink and orange hues, like the rainbow trout in the fish department of the grocery store.

It's a mermaid. A real mermaid. The tail slaps the surface of the water. Dad steadies me.

"Oh my," he breathes.

I hear Gran mutter "Selkie," and a shiver runs up my spine. It's finally happening. I'm looking at a real mermaid. Something inside me always knew I would.

I raise my hands in the air over my head, a gesture of surrender, of peace. It works. The mermaid freezes, her eyes locked with mine. I slowly make my way into the water. Dad takes my crutches and follows close behind me. She is tangled in weeds, getting tighter as she thrashes. She seems strong, and I'm a bit scared, but still I reach out to pull the weeds from her tail … when she grabs my arm. A scream from behind me causes her to pull away. I spin around to see Mom watching from the shore. I didn't even notice she hadn't waded in with Dad and me. Her body is rigid in Grampa's arms as he holds her back.

"She's all right, Beth," he says to her gently.

"But—" Her eyes are frantic, but she lets Grampa hold her.

"I've got this," Dad says to her. Then looks at me and back to Mom. "Actually, *she's* got this. Go ahead, Meranda. She trusts you. She'll let you help her now," he says, gesturing toward the creature.

I look back at the mermaid, trying to take her in. Her face is round and her skin almost translucent against her tangled black hair. She would look almost human if it weren't for the dark, bulging, fish-like eyes continually scanning her surroundings and the wide mouth stretching across most of her face. Shimmering scales cover her chest and arms and trail off at the base of her neck. She reaches out slowly to take my arm again. I let her. I don't feel so scared anymore, and I watch as she turns my arm over in her hand and traces the outline of my birthmark with her long webbed fingers. Then her hand moves to my face, her scales sliding against my cheek gently. Her body relaxes suddenly, and her arm drops into the water as she slumps over. She has fainted. I see now that the water around her is red with blood. She's hurt.

"Mom! She needs help!" I call frantically, struggling to support the mermaid's head as she slouches in my arms. Dad comes forward, and we work to free her body from the weeds.

"I'll get your bag." I look up to see Grampa running back to the truck, and Mom wading into the water toward us. But she stops behind me, staring blankly ahead. She looks lost.

"Mom," I yell. "She's bleeding. She needs your help."

My words flip a switch in Mom.

"It's on the floor by my seat, Dad," she yells back to Grampa. Suddenly, she is Dr. Morgan, moving efficiently and quickly. The three of us free the unconscious mermaid from the tangles of weeds.

"We need to get her onto the shore," she orders. "Here, support her tail so I can get her up."

I move my arms under the enormous appendage. The scales are smooth, sliding along my icy skin. We struggle together to drag her onto the sand, her limp body slippery in our hands. On the shore, Mom and Dad lay the mermaid down as I stand at the water's edge, watching, my heart in my throat. Mom kneels beside her and begins to examine the large cut through the scales on her torso when Grampa returns with her bag.

"There are a few packages of sutures in the side pocket." Mom holds out her hand so Dad can give her what she needs. There is blood pooling in the mud at Mom's knees. "Put pressure here, Gabe. I'll get the sutures ready."

While Mom is stitching the wound, Grampa comes over to help me get out of the water. I am starting to feel the fatigue from all that I've been through. So much has happened, and my body is struggling to catch up, I think.

"Quite the sight, eh? You've had a lot to take in these past few days." He gives my shoulder a squeeze as he helps me clamber onto the shore. My legs feel like anchors pulling me down. I collapse onto the cool sand, where I can watch Mom work.

"The men and women on the dock last night. They were out hunting mermaids," I say with a shudder.

Grampa nods solemnly. "Aye, looks like they got one." He sits down beside me, mesmerized by the glistening creature in front of us. "Unbelievable."

Gran stands protectively behind Mom as she stitches and snips the thread. She's quiet, but her eyes dance with wonder. She reaches to her neck and turns a delicate gold pendant over and over in her fingers. She's wearing her McKenzie necklace again.

Suddenly, the mermaid comes to with a gasp, her globe-like eyes darting between Mom and Dad and Gran and Grampa. She makes a move toward the water, clearly terrified—but then she sees me and stops flailing. I lock eyes with her, crawl closer, and reach out my hand. She takes it. I hear Mom inhale next to me, as if to speak. But she doesn't. The mermaid's scaly hand is cool in mine. She covers it with her other hand, and her wide mouth stretches into a kind of smile. I can't believe this is happening, but it also feels so real, and my eyes fill with tears. Just as I'm about to say something, to try to talk to her, she flips herself over, her tail thrusting her body back into the water. And with a massive splash, she's gone, her tail disappearing below the surface of the lake.

We all sit in silence for a moment, listening to our own thoughts. "Well, I'll be," sighs Gran eventually. "It's like that mermaid knew you." She glances knowingly at Mom.

"Do you think it was the one from—?" I look to Mom. I can see in her face that she is struggling to rewrite the memories in her mind of that awful day. She shakes her head, bewildered.

The ripples created by the mermaid's departure fade, and the lake is still again. The last pink hues of the sunset glisten on its mirrored surface. The water guards the secrets in its depths, steadfast and unchanging. But we are forever changed. I take a deep, cleansing breath, trying to inhale the beauty of this moment.

Gran breaks the silence. "Oh, my word, I've always held out hope that it wasn't true, that the mermaids hadn't turned against us."

We all look to her, startled from our trances. She's right—this changes everything.

"But now this town's turned on them," Grampa says. "I wonder if any more of them were hurt today." He sighs. "Fear can make folks do terrible things."

"We need to fix this," I say, standing, as Dad hands me my crutches. "We need to set things right." I know it won't be easy to shift the tides of people's opinions—but I hope that, little by little, they will be able to see the truth.

"I think you've already started doing that, Mer-girl," Grampa says with a wink.

LOCAL MAN RECANTS MERMAID STORY

Angus (Gus) MacDonald has revised his accounts of the deaths of Steven Kirkland and Mark McKenzie. Both men died after falling overboard from lobster vessel Stormy Skye *more than a decade apart. MacDonald had claimed he had witnessed a mermaid pull Kirkland from the deck of the boat and into the water, fuelling local legend, as well as his own tour business. MacDonald's boat was towed to shore during Sunday night's storm in a harrowing rescue by his crewmates. He immediately confessed to arguing with Kirkland before witnessing him get tangled and fall overboard. McKenzie's death has since been determined to have been caused by a heart attack. In addition to changing his statements, MacDonald also pleaded guilty to stealing from Kirkland's lobster fishing company a decade ago. He has been charged with theft and obstruction of justice; sentencing to be held this week.*

***Skye Gazette*, September 21, 2018**

10 MONTHS LATER

The twinkling reflection of the late morning sun on the lake bounces off my skin, painting a lacy, almost scaly living masterpiece on my legs. The warmth from the sun-drenched wood of the dock seeps into my body, and the sway from the gentle waves matches the rhythm of my breath. At the house, the back window is open, and I can hear Dad humming in the kitchen below the sound of running water in the sink. He curses, and I can only assume he's hit his head on the hanging cabinets. Again. We're all still getting used to the quirks of the new house. When the little place next door to Gran and Grampa's went up for sale, it was the last sign we needed. We knew where we belonged.

We moved in January, and I started school at Skye Middle School to finish off the seventh grade. Claire says it's like I've been here all my life. I guess that means I'm adjusting. She and her family are in counseling together, and her mom is getting better. Slowly. Once the snow melted, Claire and I biked to school, something Mom never would have let me do in Calgary.

Mom does shifts at the small hospital emergency department and sees pediatric consults in the clinic. Dad has perfected the art of video communication and virtual professorship with his lab back in Calgary and is back on track to cure cancer.

I see Gran and Grampa every day. Before the lake started to freeze, Grampa took me out in their boat, and I have started to memorize the shoreline that is once again my home. I've been to the ocean. I've felt the icy waves of the Atlantic splash my legs and salt mist trapped in my hair, letting me carry part of the ocean home. The photo next to my bed in my new room is of the three of us, Mom, Dad, and me, damp and shivering under a wool blanket after my first icy dip. The look on Mom's face is priceless; she's laughing so hard, with tears in her sparkling eyes.

The legends of Skye continue to thrive. I am once more a sort of celebrity. "McKenzie girl saved again by mermaids," they say. I don't correct them, but Dad sure does. He tells anyone who will listen about his daughter, the hero of the lake. I'm not sure anyone believes him.

My "fame" gave me a platform to help reframe Skye's mermaid legends. Claire and Howard from the *Gazette* helped me research timelines and witness statements from the accidents and misadventures blamed on mermaid attacks over the years since Steven Kirkland's death. When viewed with fresh eyes—and less fear—it turns out all of them had very real, non-mythical explanations. Howard was so impressed, he asked me to write an article for the paper.

Gus's official statement was taken by Detective Sullivan. He was sentenced to probation and community service for obstruction of justice and theft, and at Gran's and Sarah's insistence, he maintains the new fisherman's monument on the pier. Between my work and Gus's confession, hope and magic have returned to Skye. The statue at the post office has been repaired and has become a bit of a tourist destination again. The ripples of fear and distrust that had begun with Gus's lies had caused a fracture in the remarkable relationship between Skye and the mermaids, and now, the healing has begun. Even Sarah Chapman has come around. She's writing an updated edition of the *Legends* book and has asked Gran to contribute a chapter about the McKenzies.

The dock creaks.

"Hi, honey." It's Mom. She sits down next to me, facing the lake. "What a beautiful morning."

"How'd your appointment go?" I ask her.

"Fine. Hard." She sighs. "Seems that my fears run deep, but my therapist says that if we call them out, that helps them shrink. And it's getting a bit easier day by day." She pats my hand. "After all, in the wise words of Anne Shirley, 'Tomorrow is a new day, with no mistakes in it …'"

"'YET!'" we say together and laugh at one of our favorite quotes.

"Seeing you here, on the dock, exactly where you belong, I remember what is important. And what I kept you from for so long. That is what keeps me going back for help. You make me stronger, Meranda."

SLAP!

We both sit up. The dock sways. We scan the water. There it is. A glittering tail breaks the surface, then *SLAP!* Another. And another. Like fireworks of scales, sunshine and droplets of water. Then next to me by the dock, a mermaid reaches toward me. Her dark eyes smile and sparkle like the surface of the lake. I take her hand, then look back to Mom. I still can't get used to this. Mom smiles at me. She puts her hand over ours.

"We McKenzies have mermaids in our history and water in our blood," she says, gently touching the gold pendant at the base of my neck. She had her necklace repaired for me, and I haven't taken it off since. "And your name. It was no typo, you know. It was always meant to be. Mer-anda, for the sea."

I dangle my feet into the water, grip the mermaid's arm, and slip in, leaving my crutches behind. Every inch of me is alive and light in the cool water. Will I ever get used to how this feels? We make our way across the surface of the lake, me kicking my legs as hard as I can, flanked by more tails and splashes. I look back at the dock. Mom stands watching, our perfect house on the hill behind her. She blows me a kiss, smiling. The silhouette of her waving her arms gets smaller and smaller.

My heart races with the thrill of the water, and it is full with the truth that Mom will be there when I get back, ready to wrap her strong arms around me. And just as ready to let go.

ACKNOWLEDGMENTS

The journey to holding this book in my hands has been a long one, filled with twists and detours (including medical school!). Resurrecting my childhood dream of becoming an author has only been possible with the support and love of many.

Thank you to my agent, Elizabeth Bennett, who believed in this book and found it a home with the wonderful team at Owlkids. To Owlkids editors Karen Li and Sarah Howden, whose vision and skill not only elevated my story and my words to unimaginable heights but somehow made the revision and editing process even more fun than writing the original drafts.

Thanks to Dr. Lee Burkholder, who helped ensure Meranda's physical abilities were celebrated by talking me through equipment adaptations and sharing his experiences with patients' boundless goals and accomplishments.

To Laurie Lee, whose initial praise (and surprise!) planted the seed that led to my pursuit of publication. And who, along with Mary Fras, read and reread and helped work out plot challenges while dodging the ever-looming threat of cartoon mermaids. You have both been such patient champions, and I am so lucky to have you in my corner.

I am forever grateful to my parents, Bob and Susan Hamel, whose love and support showed me that I could achieve anything (and apparently, everything) I worked for.

My children were the spark that reignited my long-buried love of literature and writing. Grace's passion for reading drew me into each book with her, Jack's fascination with poetry propelled me to play with words again, and Abigail's bedtime snuggles continue to fill my heart to the brim. I achieved this dream because of the three of you. Thank you.

And finally, to my husband and best friend, Doug. Thank you for supporting me in adding a writing career to our already jam-packed life! You have always had my back, gently nudging me forward in the most loving way, and see the very best in me. Because, in the words of the great Alistair MacLeod, "All of us are better when we are loved." And I know I am.